NATHAN
BOY OF CAPERNAUM

NATHAN
BOY OF CAPERNAUM

By

Amy Morris Lillie

Illustrated by
Nedda Walker

New York
E. P. Dutton & Co., Inc.

TO

LAURENCE, MARY *and* HUBERT

TABLE OF CONTENTS

LIST OF ILLUSTRATIONS

FOREWORD

THERE must have been children in the crowd which surged out of the towns and cities of Galilee one spring afternoon to seek a Healer who had been doing great works of mercy throughout their land. I think there may have been a boy who started to follow the crowd, and then outran the rest and came first to the slope of the hill where Jesus sat with his disciples looking down on the city of Capernaum and the blue waters of his beloved Sea of Galilee.

If there had been such a boy, he probably would have crept behind a bush or rock where he could quietly watch and listen, for children in Palestine did not push themselves forward in any gathering of older people. So, half hidden, he might have heard for the first time the voice of Jesus, and witnessed the approach of that multitude which ran and scrambled up the hillside to the Master's feet and then listened so eagerly as he talked to them of a kind of happiness which was new and startling. So, too, such a boy might have absorbed the truths of Jesus's teaching, even though he did not understand them fully, and later found them knocking at the doors of his heart and mind as he followed the pattern of his daily life.

Foreword

In this story, NATHAN, BOY OF CAPERNAUM, I have tried to recapture the feelings and emotions awakened in a thoughtful Palestinian boy of ten by the influences radiating from the presence of Jesus in his community, and his application of the teaching of Jesus to his own small problems. Against the background of a devout Jewish family, Nathan leads the life of an average boy of his time, but his eyes and ears are ever alert to the activities and conversations of fishermen on the shore or merchants in the market place. His mother is a kinswoman of Andrew and Simon Peter, thus Nathan finds it easy to follow the comings and goings of Jesus and his disciples, particularly since his parents had become friends and followers of the Master through the healing of their younger son. It had been for the purpose of asking the Healer's help for this little brother, who had been crippled by a fall, that Nathan had outrun the crowd to the mountain of the Beatitudes.

The objective in writing this story has been three-fold: First, to present a picture of the life of a child in Capernaum during the brief period of Jesus's ministry there. To show the customs and activities of a busy city of that day; to give, through the incidents of the story, a glimpse into the lives of fishermen, merchants, farmers, and shepherds, as well as of the travelers whose caravans passed through this city from east, west, north and south, bringing to it news from all parts of the known world; and to show the reverent observance and significance of the Jewish feasts and seasons. In short, to make real to a child of today the world in which Jesus lived.

Second, to offer a body of moral teaching, based upon the Sermon on the Mount, which can be understood by a child because it is presented through the medium of a child's mental processes and experience. I have tried to interpret the truths of the Beatitudes as they might have been worked out in the thinking of a boy of Capernaum, and to make them mean something to modern children. The story form of the book provides incidental material which would be adaptable to many different units of study for ten-year-old children. Each chapter might be the nucleus from which an entire unit could be developed, or the book as a whole used for a more extended study unit on the Beatitudes. The eleven chapters have continuity, covering the ministry of Jesus from the time he began to teach and heal along the shores of the Sea of Galilee and made his home with his disciples in Capernaum, to the closing days of that ministry which led to Calvary and the great moments of the resurrected Christ.

The third, and perhaps the most important, purpose I have had in mind is to give children a *feeling* about Jesus. To show him a dynamic and magnetic person such as Nathan found him. One who entered into a child's fun and a child's unhappiness in Galilee, and who is mindful of children today in just the same terms. Unless a child can by imagination project

Foreword

himself into the scenes or situations possible in those Galilean days, the life of Jesus as lived two thousand years ago can have little reality for him. For this reason I have used fictitious characters in an authentic Biblical setting, feeling that people and families such as these surely lived in Capernaum, and that by giving them names and relationships a child will more readily associate himself with the story than if Nathan were described as a little boy, Simeon a farmer, or Benjamin a shepherd, and so on. This imaginary form has been used many times, for how can a child or adult arrive at any appreciation or understanding of the life of Jesus without the wings of the imagination to fill out the limited records of the Gospels? As the final verse of St. John's Gospel says: "And there are also many other things which Jesus did, the which, if they should be written every one, I suppose that even the world itself could not contain the books that should be written." Teaching the events of the life of Jesus to children is not very fruitful unless they can be given a *real feeling* about him which will grow to express itself in a warm and spontaneous emotion. I have endeavored to picture Jesus as a boy of Capernaum might have seen him and learned to adore him. If any boy or girl today should be led, through this little book, to the same vision and love, its purpose will have been fulfilled.

A. M. L.

Chapter 1

FOLLOWING THE CROWD

"He went up into a mountain"

LITTLE waves were sending bright foam nearly to his feet as Nathan raced along the shore of the Sea of Galilee. Many boats were beached or tied at their quays after a day's fishing. They belonged to the fishermen of Capernaum, the fine, busy city in which Nathan lived. Usually he would have stopped to peek into them, or waited around for the return of other boats. Nathan liked to see a good catch of fish, all silvery in the sunlight, and was always ready to give a hand in stretching the nets to dry if the men would let him. But today he wanted only to follow a little crowd of people which he had seen moving along a road. This road, Nathan knew, led to the hills which rose, high and steep, in back of the city.

It was fun to follow a crowd. Sometimes it led to a wedding, where flutes, tambourines and drums made music in the streets for dancing. Or it might be a funeral, where the mourners made almost as much noise. Then there were times when someone had been guilty of breaking the law and was being led off for punishment. There were even times when such people were chased out of town. But today it was a different kind of crowd. The people were not laughing or weeping, and they were not angry or cruel. Nathan had seen them pass his father's house a short time before, and many of them were sick, some so helpless that they had to be carried. They were mostly sad-looking people and very quiet as they walked along, but Nathan could see that they were trying to hurry. It seemed as though they were afraid of being late for something. He had watched until they were nearly out of sight and then had started to run after them.

Nathan was ten years old and could run pretty fast. He expected his sister Renah, who was twelve, to catch sight of him and call him back so he did not lose any time in getting beyond hearing. Renah was busy with work inside the house while their mother was praying at the synagogue for little Enoch who had fallen from a tree and whose legs, it was feared, would never be of any use to him again. Nathan thought of this sadly as his own sturdy legs raced along the shore.

It was not long before he caught up with others who, like him, had seen the crowd of people moving toward the hills and were following them. There were children whom Nathan knew, who had stopped their play in the hope of finding something more exciting to do. None of them had any idea of where they were going and they gazed with open mouths at the sick people who were being carried, or the lame who walked on crutches and could not keep up with the rest. It was not unusual to see people like this, for there were many sick and lame and blind folk around the city. But to see them all going somewhere *together* was so strange, that the children stared.

There were, also, fishermen who were friends of Nathan's father. They walked together and talked in low voices so Nathan was unable to hear what they were saying. As they went along still other men and women came out of houses and streets and joined them. No one paid any attention to Nathan so he hurried ahead, worming his way among the older people, in an effort to get near the leaders of this straggling procession. But the farther toward the front he went, the thicker grew the crowd. Dear me, thought Nathan, they must have been pouring out of all the streets of the city; and he began to feel just a little frightened. Then he heard voices speaking loudly enough for him to understand what the men were saying.

"He asked Andrew and Simon Peter, the fishermen, to go with him," said one, "and they have left their boats at the shore while they travel about the country with him."

"Yes," said another, "and James and John, the sons of Zebedee, are also of their company."

Nathan pricked up his ears for he had heard something of this at home. Simon Peter and Andrew were kinsfolk, his mother's cousins, and they had talked one evening to his parents about a newcomer to Capernaum. Peter had been very much excited and his voice had boomed all over the street so that the neighbors had been drawn to their doorway in surprise. There was a name he had mentioned — Nathan wrinkled his forehead and tried to remember. Yes, it was Jesus, of Nazareth the hill country, Peter had told them. Nathan remembered, too, some talk of a kingdom, but that was an old word. There was always talk about a new kingdom of Israel. So Nathan had gone very obediently to his sleeping mat in the corner when his mother had bidden him, and he had fallen asleep to the sound of many voices and had forgotten all about it until this moment. He trotted along beside the two men who were speaking. They did not notice as he pressed against them, for the crowd was getting thicker and all were drawn together more closely.

"There are others that have left their work besides these fishermen," said the first. "Philip and Nathaniel of Cana; and they say Matthew, the tax collector, gave up his place to someone else while he went with them."

"How will they live while they go around preaching and teaching instead of working?" asked the second fisherman.

Following the Crowd

"The sea is full of fish and they can still find food. They seem to have few wants."

"But the people who follow have plenty of wants. They have heard that he heals the sick, and they will not let him alone."

"Yes, this crowd has been disappointed because he went off to the hills today, and now they are going to find him. We'll see what this healer will do for them."

Healer! Nathan thought of his little brother, Enoch. He would tell Jesus of Nazareth about him. He would hurry and find him ahead of the crowd. Not until he had twisted through the moving throng and out of the road to the open fields, did Nathan remember that he did not know where to go. But the hills were as familiar to him as to the sheep and goats of Galilee, so he felt sure that if he kept a sharp look-out he would be able to find the Healer and his friends. Out of the road it was easier to get along. The sand and pebbles had burned his feet, but in the fields it felt cooler. The bright flowers churned about his brown legs as he broke into a run. This way, he thought, he could strike one of the sheep or goat trails that wound over the hills, and he might find the Healer before the weary travelers on the road should reach him.

When Nathan had climbed until his breath came fast and his knees shook a little, he stopped and turned to look back at the city which lay in the shadow of the hills. Beyond, the Sea of Galilee reached as far as he could see. Fishing boats were making their way slowly to shore, their sails slack in a falling wind. Capernaum was only one of several lovely cities on this lake, but Nathan thought it was the most beautiful. As he turned to climb again, his breath suddenly caught in his throat. Not far from where he stood, a little company of men was sitting on the grassy slope. Nathan saw Andrew and Peter so he knew he had found the Healer. He dropped to his knees behind a bush for he was afraid they would not let him stay if they saw him, although it was plain that all were listening very intently to the one who was speaking. Nathan could not hear the voice of the speaker, but he could catch a glimpse of his face and could see that his lips were moving. The last rays of the sun coming over the top of the hill fell on his head. It made him look all shining, Nathan thought, and he began to wriggle forward on his hands and knees, moving as softly as a little animal from bush to rock and rock to bush, until he was near enough to hear what was being said.

For a few moments he lay still, behind a rock where he could have reached out and touched Andrew's shoulder. Now he could hear clearly, but his ears did not seem to take in words so much as the sound of the voice which was speaking. There were tones in it that made Nathan think of all the lovely sounds of earth which he knew so well; the wind, the sea, bells, and a sudden rush of wings when he surprised a flock of birds. Nathan did not say or even think this to himself in words, but he felt the same wonder and delight that these sounds always brought him, as he listened to Jesus's voice. It was so different from the voices he knew that, when Peter asked a question, he felt as though he had dropped from some high place with a bump. He sat up suddenly and gazed at the men.

Andrew was pointing down the hill and all had turned to look, except Peter who faced Jesus and whose angry voice had asked the question which had startled Nathan. And now Nathan knew what he meant by his question. He saw, as his eyes followed Andrew's pointing finger, that the valley and hills below were full of people climbing and scrambling up the slopes, for those in the lead had discovered Jesus and his friends.

"Master," Peter had cried, "see how they come after you and will not let you rest. Go still farther into the hills. We will send them back!"

Nathan looked quickly back at Jesus, for the voice he already loved was answering Peter: "No, Peter, let them come." And then Jesus began to talk of happiness. His eyes were looking toward the climbing people but they seemed to Nathan to be seeing beyond them, far, far out over the Sea of Galilee, and his face was the kindest face Nathan had ever seen. He was talking of a happiness that sounded strange to Nathan, and even the fishermen looked puzzled; a happiness which was not for the proud and rich but for the humble and poor, the sad, and those whom Nathan had been taught to despise. Even the hungry should be happy because they would be fed. And he spoke of kindness, of those who showed mercy, and of making peace instead of war. There were promises, too; something about the Kingdom of Heaven which would belong to these people.

It was all very confusing to Nathan, who knew only about the kingdom which would one day be returned to his people; a kingdom for which they prayed in the synagogue. How, he wondered, could a kingdom of any kind come without a great king or leader who would gather together all the proud and mighty men of the land and go forth to battle as the heroes of Israel had done in the past?

The crowd was close now and was pressing forward to hear what Jesus was saying. Nathan was afraid they would push between him and the friends who had drawn closer around their Master, so he forgot his fear of being discovered and wriggled right in between Peter and Andrew. But Peter's strong hand came down heavily on his shoulder and Nathan was caught before he could thrust himself into the circle.

"What are you doing here?" asked Peter, not recognizing him at first. "This is no place for children."

"Let me stay," whimpered Nathan. "I want to tell the Healer about little Enoch."

"You are young Nathan," said Peter in surprise, and not unkindly, "but you must not bother the Master. You must go home." He gave the boy a push and Nathan put his hand up to his eyes, for he felt he could not bear the disappointment. Then he heard Jesus speaking to Peter.

"Don't send him away, Peter. Never keep the children away from me." And he held out his hands to Nathan, and to other children who were trying to edge closer, their eyes big with curiosity. Free now of those who had held them back, they went shyly but eagerly and stood beside Jesus or sat at his knee. "Would you learn the secret of happiness, also, little ones?" Jesus asked with a smile. Then he said to the men: "It is of such as these that the Kingdom of Heaven is built. Except all of you shall have the heart of a child you shall not be able to enter into it."

Nathan felt warm and happy. He had something to do with this new kingdom, then. He could not understand all that the Master was saying, but just to listen to his voice and look up into his eyes that seemed to be seeing everything and every one, this was enough for him.

When Nathan looked at the crowd he could see that there were many kinds of people besides the sick. There were rulers of the synagogue who, Nathan knew, had come to report what they saw to those who kept the Books of the Law, so they might decide whether this healer was keeping the Sacred Law. There were other men, too, belonging to the rich people of Capernaum. Nathan suspected some had come to laugh and have fun. But, if their mouths were open, they did not seem to be laughing.

Most of the faces which Nathan saw were anxious, hungry faces. They needed help so much, and yet they were patient and quiet. The sick, who had managed to crawl or be carried near enough, lay on the grass exhausted from the long climb. Others, the lame and blind, leaned against their guides for a time and then slid to the grass where they could rest while they listened. There seemed to be healing even in the voice of the Healer and in the words he spoke, thought Nathan, as he saw how faces changed before his eyes. He could not have told how it happened or just what it was he saw, but it reminded him of the way dark windows became bright when the candles were lighted within the houses in Capernaum.

And now the Healer was getting up and gently putting aside Nathan and the other children as he moved toward the people. The crowd closed in around him and Peter gripped Nathan by the arm and told him he would go back part way to town with him. The Master, he said, would be busy until dark, and none could hold him back from this work of healing the poor sick bodies of all who came to him for help. Peter shook his big curly head and frowned as he said this, so Nathan asked him if he did not like to have people made well.

"Yes," said Peter, "but they are after him all the time and he gets no rest. It is more than bodies he has come to cure, little Nathan. There, you would not understand, so say no more about it. Come now," and Peter led the way around the edges of the crowd down toward the town.

What, wondered Nathan, could be more important than bodies? What else could be made well? What else was sick besides bodies? He was disappointed that he could not have stayed to see the Healer work his magical cures, and to tell him about his little brother, Enoch. But he knew there was no arguing with Peter, or even talking to him, when he was in this mood. So he followed along quietly, remembering a kind beautiful face and the sound of a voice he could never forget, a voice telling people how to be happy.

Chapter ii

ON THE ROOF-TOP

"Happy the poor in spirit"

NATHAN left Peter by the shore where his boat was tied. Other fishermen had come in with their catch of fish and Peter wanted to talk with them. They could tell him whether there were fish in the shallow water which he could catch with a small net, or whether he and Andrew would have to take their boat out into deep water and fish during the night. Peter's family lived in a little house close to the shore. He had been away from them for several weeks and now he must start to provide food for them again. Nathan wanted to stop and listen to the fishermen talk, but Peter pointed to the long shadows and warned him that his mother would be expecting him home for the evening meal.

Speaking of the evening meal made Nathan feel that some warm bread from his mother's oven, and perhaps a little cake with fresh goat's milk, would taste good. There would be dates and figs, too, dried in the sun on the roof of his home. He sometimes spread the fruit there himself to help his mother. So Nathan said goodbye to Peter and raced off toward the small white house where he lived with his father, mother, sister Renah, and his five-year-old brother, Enoch.

Nathan's father was not a fisherman. He was a farmer whose farm was about a mile from the city. Farmers often slept in their fields when the crops were ripe, to keep from being robbed. Then came the threshing. Wheat and barley had to be cut down and the good part separated from the straw or husks. It took a long time for the crops to be threshed and put into barns where they would be safe, so Nathan's father and his helpers slept in the fields instead of going home at night.

The threshing season was now well advanced, and Nathan remembered it had been his turn tonight to take supper to his father. He ran as fast as he could and soon reached home. From the doorway came the warm odor of fresh baked bread, but no one was inside. Nathan had not expected to find anyone there, as the family lived most of the time on the roof-top where it was cooler in warm weather. They even slept there, and Nathan loved the nights with only the stars overhead.

Tonight he found his mother with Enoch, who was

dipping his little cake into a cup of milk with a great show of appetite. Anna, Nathan's mother, sat on a mat with the little boy beside her. His helpless legs were stretched out in front of him like a rag doll's. Anna's eyes were turned toward the hills and Nathan saw her lips moving. He felt she must be saying one of her favorite verses from the Book of Praise. Usually when she looked that way she was saying: "I will lift up mine eyes unto the hills, from whence cometh my help." Nathan's heart jumped as he remembered what he had seen and heard in the hills. Perhaps help would come very soon.

Enoch cried out with joy when he saw Nathan, and his mother turned her head. "Where have you been, my son?" she asked. "It was getting late and Renah had to go to the fields with food for your father and his helpers. Was it not your task?"

Nathan hung his head a moment. Then he threw himself down beside his mother. "I followed after a crowd of sick people, Mother," he said. "They were going into the hills to find a healer who could cure them. I ran ahead and found him first. He was with our kinsmen, Andrew and Peter, and others. I thought of Enoch ——"

"Ah — healers," sighed Anna, "I have been to healers but they do not help. No, it is from God alone my help must come."

"But, Mother," pleaded Nathan, "this healer is different. I saw . . ." and then Nathan stopped because he had not seen changed bodies; he had seen only changed faces. Peter had made him come home.

26

On the Roof-top

"You saw what?" asked his mother with more interest.

"I saw his face, Mother. I was as close to him as I am to you, and his face was — true. He would do what he said he would, I know it. And he wants people to be happy."

Anna looked at Nathan's flushed cheeks and bright eyes. Then understanding came into her face. "You must be speaking of Jesus of Nazareth. He is back, then, and Peter and Andrew with him. I have heard of his great works in Galilee since they went off together. You must tell me, Nathan, how he spoke. But first take your bread and milk. Shall we let him have some fruit and a little cake, Enoch, since he is not as naughty as we feared?"

"Yes, yes," shouted Enoch joyfully. So Nathan ate his supper and thought it had never tasted so good. But he did not try to make it last as long as possible, as he sometimes did, for he was eager to tell his mother all that had happened that afternoon.

Anna was a good mother. She always had time to listen to her children. Perhaps one reason was that she did not have as large a family as most of her neighbors. Her home had been saddened by the loss of two children, one a boy, older than Nathan, and the other a little daughter; and now Anna felt that the accident to her youngest son, Enoch, might mean that God was angry and was punishing her for some fault. Nathan had not seen his mother smile for many weeks although she was always kind and patient. He knew how pretty her face was when she smiled, because he re-membered her laughing with the other women of the town at the well when they went for water in the evening. Now, she always sent Renah to fill the water jars. Every day she went to the synagogue to pray and offer sacrifices to God for her sin.

Nathan was very dear to his mother. He was now her oldest son, and the oldest son was important in the family. Then, too, he was such a strong, active boy, and so ready to help either at home or in the fields with his father. Soon his hands would be big enough to guide a plough or to drive the oxen around the threshing floor. Anna watched him as he ate, and lifted her heart in a prayer to God for his safety.

When Nathan had finished the last crumb, he rolled over on his stomach and propped himself up on his elbows. With his chin resting in his hands, he could look up into his mother's face. It was good to be alone with her and Enoch in the quiet of the day. Although Nathan's family did not have to share their house with other families, as many in the city did, they usually had guests. Anna and Simeon, Nathan's father, never turned a traveler from their door, so the guest room was often occupied. They were friendly, also, with the neighbors. But tonight there was no one with Anna but Nathan and little Enoch.

Nathan did not quite know how to start telling his mother about the Healer. There was so much he couldn't put into words. Anna had to urge him gently. "Tell me, my son, what did Jesus of Nazareth say?" she asked. Then Nathan found his tongue. His eyes seemed to be seeing again that group on a hillside and a man talking about happiness for those who thought they could not hope to be happy. It was a happiness which Nathan longed to see on his mother's sad face, so he tried to tell her in the best way he could, all the strange things Jesus had said and promised.

Anna listened while she gently stroked Enoch's curls as he lay in the circle of her arm. When Nathan stopped for breath her face had changed. "You thought him different from anyone else, did you not, Nathan?" she asked. Then, putting Enoch aside on his rug, she stood up. "I will go to the well for the water tonight, my son. Take care of your brother."

Nathan was disappointed that his mother had said so little about the story he had been telling her. He was surprised, too, that she was going to the well. He and Enoch watched as she placed a small round pad on her head and lifted the water jug to rest on it. Nathan thought his mother's back looked straighter and that her step was quicker as she left them to go down into the street. He had hoped he might be allowed to go down to the shore again before it became dark, or to play with the children in the street, but now he must stay with Enoch until his mother came home or Renah got back from the farm.

It was not much fun playing with Enoch. He could not run about, and had a way of wailing like a girl if Nathan didn't do what he wanted him to. It was because he was not well, of course, and Nathan felt ashamed as he looked down at his little brother whose thin face was raised so eagerly to his. Enoch wanted to hear more about the "man in the hills." "Do you think he could make my legs well, Nathan?" he asked in an anxious, piping voice. "I do wish he would."

Nathan had not a single doubt that Jesus could heal

29

Enoch, but he felt a sudden fear that Jesus might go away during the night and they would not be able to find him the next day. Why hadn't his mother taken Enoch in her arms and gone in search of the Healer this very night? He was not big enough to carry Enoch himself. Even Renah found the five-year-old boy too heavy to lift often. No, there was no way tonight, and tomorrow might be too late. Nathan's eyes turned from Enoch's pleading face to where, beyond the city, the hills were now a soft purple. God was there, his mother had said so. Perhaps He would let Jesus stay until Nathan could find him again. Nathan prayed with his eyes still on the hills. It made him feel happier.

Enoch, having received no answer to his question, had begun to cry softly. Nathan dropped down beside him on the mat. He thought that even if he could do nothing tonight about making his little brother's legs strong again, he could make his heart lighter. He took some marbles from a bag tied to his tunic. "See, Enoch," he said, "we will play marbles, and tomorrow we will find the Healer who will make you well."

Enoch's eyes were bright once more and his thin hands reached for the marbles. When Renah came, both boys were excited over their game.

Renah was not cross with Nathan as he expected she might be. She came running up the steps to tell them about an important traveler who was turning into their street. She thought he came from the East. Perhaps he was a merchant prince from Babylon or India for his skin was dark and his camels carried heavy loads. Renah was surprised to find only Nathan and Enoch on the roof. She was even more surprised to learn that her mother had gone to the well. But, by this time, they could all hear the sound of camel bells, so Nathan jumped up and ran to the side of the roof where he could look down into the street. Renah pulled Enoch's mat over to the low stone wall that ran around the edge of the roof and lifted him high enough so that he, too, could see.

People had gathered in the street or on other roof tops to look at the strangers, who had now almost reached Nathan's house. This was not by any means the first time they had seen travelers or merchants from the East, for Capernaum was an important city and lay on the way to other large cities. But the bright-colored turbans on the heads of the men who rode on their swaying camels, and the jingling of bells as they moved along, always made the townspeople think of faraway places. It filled them with wonder at a world so different from their own.

This must be a very rich traveler, Nathan thought, for he had so many camels all loaded with heavy sacks. Two men rode ahead, and others ran beside the rest of the procession to guide the camels and keep them in line. The merchant prince rode alone and he looked very proud and stern to Nathan. His turban was of gold and sparkled with gems. The robe he held around him, and the trappings on his camel, were of costly materials. What more could anyone want? Nathan wondered. And yet the traveler's face was dark and gloomy as though his pride and riches were like a heavy burden that he could not lift from his shoulders.

Enoch clapped his hands at the lovely sound of the bells

31

and then drew back as one of the camels reached up to nibble at the leaves of an olive tree in front of the house. It brought the camel's long nose a little too close. One of the runners struck it with a stick and the camel squealed and moved over into line.

"He must be going to the inn for the night," said Renah. "We may see them in the market-place tomorrow."

Nathan leaned over to watch the last of the traveler's caravan passing on up the street. A little crowd of children was following it, keeping far enough behind to be out of reach of the brown men with the sticks, who every once in a while made a move toward them and sent them scattering. Nathan did not feel like running after this procession as he had the one in the afternoon. He would rather have Renah tell some stories while he watched the long shadows spread and lengthen. Pretty soon the whole world would be one big shadow.

It was fun to lie on your back and count the first stars. Enoch's eyes were as sharp as Nathan's and the two boys sometimes made a game of it. The stars were pale and hard to find at first, but, almost while you were looking, the sky seemed to draw farther and farther away behind a dark curtain. Then, suddenly, there were so many stars you couldn't begin to count them, and the game had to be given up. If Nathan did not fall asleep, he liked to keep on looking at them as they grew brighter and clustered closer together. Sometimes he could people the sky with giant, starry figures.

Tonight Renah was kind about telling stories. The passing

of the Eastern prince made her want to tell of the glory of their own people in the past. She told about the kings of Israel. Nathan liked to hear how David, the shepherd boy, played on his harp and sang for King Saul. It was thrilling to be told that this same David later became a great king, himself.

"Renah," Nathan asked, "was David happier when he was king than he was when he was only a shepherd boy?"

Renah did not like to be interrupted by what she thought was a silly question so she said rather crossly: "Wouldn't you rather be a king than a shepherd?"

"I guess so," answered Nathan. But he did not feel sure, because it would not be the kind of happiness he had heard about that afternoon. David, the shepherd boy, would know more about that kind of happiness than David, the king. Nathan thought of the boy David on the hills of Judea with his sheep. Perhaps he lay on the ground and looked at the stars as he, Nathan, was doing. Perhaps that was how he came to sing the song which was written in the Book of Praise:

> "The heavens declare the glory of God;
> And the firmament showeth his handiwork."

Was it when he led his sheep over hills and through green valleys, bright with scarlet, white, or purple flowers, that he had discovered:

> "The earth is the Lord's, and the fullness thereof;
> The World, and they that dwell therein."

Nathan, Boy of Capernaum

David, thought Nathan, had found out that the world belonged to God — the heavens, the earth, and people. Kings thought the world belonged to them and each fought for the biggest piece of it. His own people were hoping today for a king who would win back a kingdom for Israel and drive out their Roman rulers. The Healer had talked about a kingdom, but not that kind of kingdom. He had said the Kingdom of Heaven, and he had promised it to lowly people who had no pride of power or riches. Children were part of it, Nathan remembered. Jesus had said that to Peter. Yes, David the shepherd boy had found out something that kings forgot, and it made him happier than a king. Nathan thought he would rather be out on the hills with David, and have the whole world for a kingdom because he belonged to God, than to live with David in a palace as king of Israel.

Renah's voice went on and on telling of the glory of the kings of Israel, but Nathan's eyes were closing. It was another kind of glory he was seeing on the face of a Healer on the hills behind Capernaum. Jesus of Nazareth *knew*, and he lighted candles behind the eyes of sad, hopeless people until their faces were shining. Nathan remembered for a moment the proud, dark face of the merchant from the East. There had been no happiness there. Then he saw again the face of Jesus.

Anna, Nathan's mother, came home late and found them all asleep. She lifted the water pitcher from her head and placed it in its usual corner. Then she knelt for her evening prayer. Her heart was very thankful. She had heard many

34

things at the well about Jesus of Nazareth. She had gone afterward to the house of Simon Peter, and Peter's wife had told her that Jesus would be at their house for awhile. Anna was full of hope for her little son, Enoch. Surely God had sent her the help she had asked of Him. Her lips smiled as she softly repeated words which, also, had been sung by the shepherd boy of the Judean hills:

> "O give thanks unto the Lord; for he is good.
> For his loving-kindness endureth forever."

Chapter iii

THE HEALER

"Happy the mourners"

IN THAT warm eastern country of Galilee, with its beautiful lake and busy cities, the day's work began with the sunrise. People went to sleep at night without taking off their clothes. Their beds were thick mats which could be unrolled and rolled up again in the morning very quickly. Here the sunrise came very suddenly; it flooded land, sea, and roof tops with light all at once. There was no gray dawn, such as we know, with the sky growing slowly brighter before the sun is really up. In Galilee the stars were hardly gone when the sun appeared over the eastern rim of the world, and Capernaum, that city on the Sea of

The Healer

Galilee where Nathan lived, was stirring and stretching itself for a new day.

Nathan felt the warmth of the sun tickling the soles of his bare feet and creeping along his spine as he lay sprawled out on his stomach with his face buried in his arms to keep the bright glare from hurting his eyes. In a few moments his mother would call from the little courtyard in front of the house and he would run down for his morning meal. Then he would go with other boys to school in the synagogue, which was the place for teaching as well as for prayer and worship.

The children learned their lessons by repeating after the teacher the words written in the Sacred Scrolls. These scrolls were their books. They were made of a kind of paper called parchment and were rolled on two sticks. All writing was done by hand. There were no printed books such as we have today, for printing presses were not invented until many hundreds of years later. The Sacred Scrolls were kept in a box or chest in the synagogue.

The most important was the Scroll of the Law. It was believed that God had given Moses and other great men rules which they were to write out for their people to follow in their daily lives. Children were taught from this scroll first. On it were the Ten Commandments and other laws which they would be expected to know and obey. Then there were scrolls telling the stories of heroes and leaders, of kings and prophets, who had made the history of their land great. Many of these were stories of boys who had been brave and loyal to God when they were young, and so were later chosen by Him to serve and lead their nation. There was, also, a Book of Praise. This was their song book, and the children loved to sing the beautiful songs of praise to God for His kindness and goodness to all people.

Nathan raised his head and opened one eye. Yes, his mother and Renah were gone. They were busy about their morning tasks as soon as the first rays of the sun reddened the eastern sky. Only Enoch was still sleeping. He looked little and helpless as he lay there on his mat. Then Nathan remembered his adventure of the afternoon before, when he had seen the Healer. He wondered if he were still in the hills. He must beg his mother to find out before it was too late. Perhaps she had heard something at the well last night. It was strange she had gone herself for water instead of sending Renah. Nathan jumped up and ran down the steps to the courtyard.

Under the shade of an olive tree he found his mother and Renah grinding grain into flour with a hand mill. They sat on the ground with the mill between them. It was made of two large round stones, one set upon the other. The upper stone turned upon the lower by means of a smooth stick or axle which was fastened to the center of the lower stone and passed through a hole in the upper one. With a handle on the top stone, two women could turn it round and round until the grain was ground into flour. Sometimes two neighbors used a mill together. Renah was very proud that she was now old enough to grind with her mother. They did it early in the morning or at the end of the day when the sun was not too hot in the courtyard. There was always an extra supply of flour kept in a bin, built into the wall inside the house, so they could share with a neighbor or make a few more loaves if guests arrived.

Anna had watched her young son running down the steps and was waiting for him with a smile. It seemed to Nathan that the world shone with special brightness this morning. Maybe his mother's smile had something to do with it. He stopped and gazed at her, and Anna saw the question in his eyes.

"Yes, my son," she said, "there is happiness in my heart this morning. You brought me hope last night when you told me about your Healer. Then, when I went to the fountain, I learned more about him."

Nathan ran to his mother's side and knelt down so he could look into her face. "Tell me," he begged, "is he still here?"

"He is here," answered Anna, "and it is said he may be staying in Capernaum for a time. He is at Simon Peter's house, when he rests under a roof, but they say he loves to sleep out in the hills and has never a fear of beasts or robbers. I have been telling Renah how you followed the crowd to the hills yesterday and saw him."

"Why didn't you tell me last night?" asked Renah in an injured voice.

"Because the caravan went by and we were watching it," answered Nathan, "and then you were telling stories and I went to sleep."

"Well, you did wrong to run away in the afternoon without telling me," said Renah. "I thought you were playing around the boats, and I looked for you there. It was your turn to take supper to the fields."

"Never mind, Renah," said Anna quietly, "Nathan will take the supper tonight. He was thinking of your little brother when he ran after the Healer."

Nathan thought about this for a moment. Renah was satisfied by his mother's answer, but he knew it was not the true reason he had run away in the first place. Nathan decided to be honest with his mother and Renah. "I ran after the crowd at first to see where the people were going," he admitted, "and then I heard them speak about a healer and I thought of Enoch."

Anna stopped grinding and put her hand on Nathan's cheek. "You are a brave boy, my Nathan, and will never be afraid to speak the truth. Now we will forget that you did wrong to go so far without asking leave, and will remember only that you have brought hope and happiness to your mother's heart."

"When shall we go to find the Healer, Mother?" Nathan asked eagerly.

"Listen, my son, and I will try to make you understand," Anna replied. "I talked with Peter's wife last night and I know that Jesus of Nazareth has done many wonderful things throughout Galilee. News of his healing has been carried far and wide by those whom he has helped. They could not be quiet about it for the joy that was in their hearts, even though he asked them to say nothing. Now the sick and crippled and distressed are pouring out of every city in search of him. They want so badly to be healed that they think only of their own poor bodies and forget that Jesus must need rest. Peter and his other friends are trying to protect him, but it is hard, for he has such great pity for the sick and helpless. We must not be among those who press him beyond his strength, my Nathan. We must wait patiently for a time when we shall have no fear of tiring him. The time will come — and soon — for I know that God has sent this good man to help us."

Nathan felt he could not bear to wait, and showed his disappointment by a frown between his eyes. His mother put a finger under his chin and tipped his face up to hers. "Is it so hard to be thoughtful of others, my son?" she asked, but her lips were still smiling. Nathan's face cleared, for he felt that Anna's eagerness to have Enoch well must be greater than his own, and the happiness in her face showed how sure she was that Jesus could heal him. "How shall we know the time, Mother?" he asked.

"As we go about our work as usual it will be made plain," answered Anna. "Renah, bring a cloth under the tree, and get the loaves from the oven while I go to the roof for Enoch. Nathan must be off soon to school."

Renah did not go to school. Only the boys were taught to read and write. Girls helped their mothers at home and were taught to bake, and to spin wool into yarn out of which clothes for the family were made. They learned very young to do their part in making the home life of the family comfortable and happy. Sometimes they helped in the fields and vineyards, or by gathering the olives in baskets at the time of the olive harvest. Boys went to school to learn reading and writing. Some of them became teachers or "rabbis" while others learned to be scribes who wrote letters or books for those who could not do it for themselves.

Nathan loved school, and every morning he ran off happily with his friends who were the sons of farmers, fishermen, and men of other trades in the city. The boys sat cross-legged in a circle on the floor and repeated after their teacher, until they knew them by heart, the words he read to them from the Sacred Scrolls. When they were learning to write, the teacher wrote each letter with a stick in the sand, which covered the floor, and the children copied it with one finger.

The very first of the writings in the Sacred Scrolls taught to children was called the Shema, which is a Hebrew word for "Hear" or "Listen." These were the words of the Shema:

> "Hear, O Israel:
> The Lord our God is one Lord:
> And thou shalt love the Lord thy God
> With all thine heart,
> And with all thy soul,
> And with all thy might."

Nathan had learned this verse before he started to go to school. It had been written on a piece of parchment and placed in a little box which hung on the doorpost of his home. The box was called the Mezuzah, and every Jewish household had one. Whenever anyone went in or out of the house it was touched with reverent fingers, because it held the commandment which was thought most important and most holy.

Today Nathan's thoughts were not all on his lessons, and several times the rabbi reached over to rap him lightly on the head with his stick because he was not repeating the words of the law with the rest. Nathan did not mean to be inattentive, but he kept thinking of other words — new words which he had heard spoken by Jesus of Nazareth — words which made people well and happy. He stole a glance out of the window whenever he could and let his eyes rest on the hilltops beyond the town. It seemed as though he could almost hear the voice of Jesus speaking.

"Why are you dreaming, Nathan ben Simeon?" asked the rabbi, rapping sharply with his stick. "Your thoughts are out-of-doors, perhaps, since your eyes are looking through the window instead of at me."

Nathan turned back quickly to his teacher and raised his voice louder than any of the other children as he tried to make up for his inattention. He did not want to confess where his thoughts had been. The boys had gone right on with their singsong chant and were making so much noise that the rabbi did not press Nathan for an answer. The words they were all saying together were about their native land, words that Nathan loved.

> "A land which the Lord thy God careth for;
>   The eyes of the Lord are always upon it,
>   From the beginning of the year
>   Even unto the end of the year."

Nathan, Boy of Capernaum

It must be true about God caring, thought Nathan, for the sunshine of Galilee was bright like a smile, and flowers seemed to burst into bloom as though a warm hand had been pressed gently against the earth. Yes, it was a lovely land!

As soon as the teacher let them go, Nathan and the rest of the boys were out through the open door as quickly as possible. They had their balls and marbles, and their voices were shrill with the excitement of being free to stretch cramped legs and arms. No wonder they sometimes came very close to quarreling about what they should do first. Some wanted to play one game and some another, and some just wouldn't play either but wanted to do something else. There were often angry voices as the boys overflowed into the market place and each tried to make his own wishes decide the kind of game a group should play.

It was that way today, and Nathan did his share of pushing and shouting for a few moments. Then he drew off to catch his breath and to look around at the storekeepers or merchants who were selling their goods in front of the shops. There was always something new and exciting to see in the market place. Farmers came with flowers and vegetables, fishermen with fish, and the shops or bazaars sold everything, from silver ornaments and brass or copper pitchers, bowls, and candlesticks, to rugs and other costly things brought from the East. Nathan thought he might see the rich merchant with his caravan who had passed his home the night before. His eyes searched the crowd of people who were buying and selling. No, there was no trace of the stranger, so Nathan decided he must have been one of those who constantly passed through Capernaum on their way to other cities.

Then Nathan's eyes opened wide and his heart began to beat faster. Standing in the shadow of a doorway, not far from him, was the Healer who had been so much in his thoughts. He was alone and stood quietly watching the antics of the children. There was a smile on his face. Nathan wondered, uncomfortably, whether he had seen the quarreling and bad temper. He could not imagine anything being missed by those eyes. He wanted to tell Jesus he was sorry for his part in it. Nathan's feet began to carry him slowly toward the Healer. It was as though he were being drawn by a string, like a little wooden toy on wheels.

When he had come close, Jesus held out his hand and Nathan ran to him. "Do you not wish to play, my son?" Jesus asked him.

Nathan shook his head. "Everyone wants to do something different," he said, and he felt ashamed as he said it.

"It takes unselfishness and good nature to be a good playmate," Jesus said kindly. "Always remember that and you will play happily. Will you walk a little way with me?" he asked, smiling down at Nathan, "I am Jesus of Nazareth, a teacher."

Nathan felt his heart grow lighter and he knew he was forgiven for his fault. He skipped along beside Jesus as they moved out of the noise of the market place into a quiet street. It was strange, thought Nathan, that no one had noticed the Healer. Perhaps he had been out in the hills all night by himself and was on his way back to Peter's house.

Nathan, Boy of Capernaum

Would this be a good time to speak of little Enoch? His mother had said the right time would be made plain if they went about their work as usual instead of searching for the Healer. Nathan looked up at Jesus but he saw that his eyes were following the flight of a flock of birds.

"Look, child," Jesus said, as he pointed after them. "Are not two sparrows sold for a farthing in the market place? Yet not one of them will fall to the ground unless your Father wills it."

"My father?" asked Nathan, wondering how his father could keep birds from falling out of the air if they were hit by a well-aimed stone from a boy's slingshot.

"Your Father, God," answered Jesus. "He cares for all small creatures. How much more, then," he added softly, "must He care for His children."

It gave Nathan a warm, safe feeling to think of God as his Father, but he felt he had to ask Jesus why God had let poor little Enoch fall from the tree and hurt his back on the stones of the courtyard. Before he knew it, Nathan had poured out the whole story.

When he had finished, Jesus said quietly: "He was such a small boy to be up in a tree. Did he try to follow you, my son?"

How had the Healer guessed it? No one, not even his mother, had blamed Nathan for Enoch's accident, but Nathan knew the little fellow had tried to reach him as he hid in the branches of the old olive tree in their courtyard.

Without waiting for an answer, Jesus went on talking. "God often entrusts the care of his small, helpless creatures to those who are able to see that no harm comes to them. If harm does come, then someone has failed God's trust in him and there is sorrow and suffering. God is sorry, too. Our Father wants His children to be happy. It was not His will that you should hide among the leaves and forget that your little brother's legs were too short to follow you with safety. That was your will, was it not?"

Nathan looked down at his dusty feet, and big tears gathered in his eyes. He swallowed hard. How could he ask Jesus to help Enoch now that he knew that he, Nathan, had been to blame?

"Where is your house, my son?" asked Jesus after a moment's silence. "Will you give me a drink of water and let me rest under your tree for a time?"

Nathan's gladness flooded his face like sunlight through an April shower. "Will you come with me," he cried, "when you know I have not been a good boy?"

"I know you have a loving heart," Jesus answered quietly, "and the other things you will learn."

They found Anna spinning in the doorway of her house. The sun was hot on the roof and she had found a shady spot for Enoch under a tree, where he played with a toy while his mother sat in the shelter of the doorway. Renah had gone to a neighbor's house on an errand for Anna. The sun was in her eyes so Anna did not know who was with Nathan at first. She saw only a tall stranger who, she thought, was a traveler wishing to rest. She rose to make him welcome.

Nathan ran to his mother. "Mother, it is Jesus of Nazareth," he cried.

Anna put her hand to her side and dropped the spindle with which she had been working. Her face was beautiful, thought Nathan, as she went forward and knelt before Jesus. "Welcome, Jesus of Nazareth," she said, "I have heard of you from my kinsmen, Simon Peter and Andrew."

Jesus laid a hand on her head. "They are my dear friends," he answered. Then very gently he helped her to her feet. "Will you give me a cup of water and let me rest here under the tree? I have walked a long way."

Anna hurried for the water jar while she told Nathan to get a bowl of water to rinse the dust from Jesus's feet. There must also be some wine and cakes.

As Nathan and his mother were busy about these things, Jesus sat down under the tree and took Enoch into his lap. When they brought the water Enoch was laughing happily over a story Jesus had been telling him. Nathan knelt to loosen the sandals and bathe the Healer's hot, tired feet. He had done this for other honored guests, but never so gladly as now. After Anna had placed a dish with some cakes, and a cup of wine made from the grapes of their own vineyard, near his hand, they sat in the shade of the tree while Jesus told them of his home in the hill country, and of his mother and brothers and sisters in Nazareth.

Nathan felt again the magic of his voice as he had felt it on the hillside. Then he began to notice Jesus's hands as they moved gently down Enoch's back or along his little helpless legs while he talked. They were strong hands and browned by the sun. As Jesus told of his work in the carpenter shop, Nathan thought that his hands would be able

48

to cut and shape the toughest wood. But they were not clumsy hands like those he had seen among the workers in the fields or in the fishing boats. They seemed to be full of life and movement. Nathan remembered a dove he had once caught and how he could feel its breast beating against his hands as though something inside it were knocking to get out, something which was part of the air and sky. When he let it go how quickly it had risen and wheeled off into the blue.

Jesus's hands made Nathan think of that dove. They gave him the feeling of something hidden and alive waiting to be released by his touch. He watched them, fascinated, wondering if Jesus held his healing in his hands as he, Nathan, had held the dove. Oh, if only he would put life and movement into the body of little Enoch!

Jesus was not talking now and Nathan raised his eyes to his face. Jesus was looking at Anna and his face was full of tenderness. "What is it that you wish, my daughter?" he asked.

Anna clasped her hands together so hard that the knuckles were white. "Lord," she said, and her voice was a whisper, as though she had no breath, thought Nathan. "Lord, that my boy may walk again like a man child and not creep like a baby all his life!"

Jesus smiled at Anna and then turned his eyes to the hills a moment. His hands were resting on Enoch's knees. Nathan thought the lump in his throat would choke him, and he wanted to cry out and beg of Jesus that he would do as his mother had asked. Then Jesus lifted Enoch and put him on his feet. "Show your mother that you can walk, little one," he said. Anna reached out to catch him if he fell, but Enoch did not fall. Instead, he stood still a moment as though surprised to find himself on his feet, and then ran to his mother and hid his face in her neck.

"Master, Master," cried Anna, and the tears were wet on her cheeks but her eyes were shining, "you have made me very happy this day!"

"Are you happier than if you had never been sad?" asked Jesus.

Nathan could not help crying out with his mother: "Yes, oh yes."

"Sorrow is like that," said Jesus. "Happy are they who have suffered, for their joy will be greater, and they will know how to comfort others."

Before Anna could loosen Enoch's arms around her neck and get to her feet Jesus was gone. Even Nathan, when he had caught his breath and raced out into the street, could not see which way he had taken.

Chapter iv

THE FARM

"Happy the gentle"

SIMEON BEN ELI, Nathan's father, was resting after a hard day of threshing the grain on his farm. He lay on a pile of straw which had been separated from the good heads of wheat and thrown to one side. All day Simeon's helpers had loaded bundles or sheaves of freshly cut grain on the backs of small donkeys which carried them to the threshing floor. Here Simeon untied the sheaves and spread them over a hard, flat piece of ground. Then a pair of oxen dragged a heavy wooden slab or platform round and round this threshing floor until grain and straw were crushed and broken. After that the good grain had to be separated from the straw by winnowing. This meant lifting shovels full of the mixed grain and straw and throwing it into the air. The breeze would blow away bits of chaff which were no good, and the straw would fall to one side. The grain was heavier and would drop at the feet of the winnower.

Sometimes women and girls helped the men in the fields, and often children would run along beside the oxen or ride on the threshing drag with the man who was driving the oxen. Nathan loved to help in the fields, and sometimes ran out to his father's farm after school. Simeon had not seen Nathan for three days. The night before, Renah had come in his place, and now it was again time for someone to be coming with supper. Simeon turned his eyes toward the road which led out from the city. Far away he could see a child running. Yes, it must be Nathan. Ah, how good it was that he had one son who was strong.

Nathan felt he could not wait to tell his father all that had happened. Anna had said he must bring his father back so he could see for himself how Enoch was walking again. It seemed like a dream, that afternoon. Soon after Jesus had slipped away, and before Anna had risen from her knees, Renah had come home to find Enoch standing on two sturdy legs. She had stopped short, and Nathan laughed aloud as he remembered how her mouth had fallen open as she stood in speechless wonder. But Renah's voice was not gone for long. Soon her cries of excitement had drawn the neighbors, and there had been great rejoicing and much curiosity about the Healer. At last, Anna had taken her little son into the house and had made him rest on a soft rug for fear so much confusion would tire him. Then she had said to the neighbors: "Do not say too much about this or the child will be a mark for those who are curious. Besides, it might increase the crowds following the Healer and drive him out of the city."

The neighbors had gone back to their homes after a good deal of talking among themselves which Nathan did not understand or listen to very much. He had been in a hurry for his mother to pack a basket with food so he could take it to the fields and tell his father the glad news. So now, at last, he was running along the dusty road until he should come to the path which would lead into the open fields of his father's farm. He knew the men would have stopped work by this time and would be resting while they waited for their supper. How good it would taste to them! Nathan stopped a moment and looked at the contents of his basket to see if his hurry had done any harm. Anna had covered everything with cool, green fig leaves to keep out the sun and dust. Nathan lifted one or two leaves and was glad to see that the round, flat loaves of bread were snug in the bottom of the basket, while some salted fish and a bowl of goat's milk cheese had not been disturbed. The olives and figs on top were all right, too, so he quickly replaced the leaves and sped on.

Nathan's father, watching his approach, wondered what made the boy in such a hurry tonight. It was a little later than usual, and a sudden fear made Simeon sit up. Perhaps something had gone wrong at home. But, as Nathan came nearer, his father could see that his face was happy, so he forgot his alarm and waited. It was easy to see that the boy had news of some kind.

Nathan was out of breath from running by the time he reached his father, and his forehead was wet with perspiration. He sat down and wiped it off with the back of his hand. It was a minute before he could speak. Simeon was sure now that it was not bad news Nathan brought so he smiled and said kindly: "Slowly, slowly, my lad. Why all this haste? Did you think we should die of hunger before the supper got here? You are late tonight but not as late as that."

Nathan drew his first long breath and then burst out: "It's about Enoch, Father. He can walk."

Simeon leaned forward and put his hand so heavily on Nathan's shoulder that it hurt. "Think what you say, boy," he said, giving him a little shake. "Has the heat gone to your head? Enoch will never stand again."

Nathan squirmed away from his father's hand. "I am telling the truth," he cried. "It was the Healer — Jesus of Nazareth."

"Ah, Jesus of Nazareth," said Simeon slowly. "It is true,

then, what I have heard about him. He is in Capernaum, and has healed your brother you say, Nathan?"

"Yes, truly he has. And my mother wants you to come and see for yourself what has happened, when you have eaten your supper."

"Call Asa and Joseph, then. They have taken the oxen and donkeys to pasture them for the night. We must eat quickly if I am to go back home with you and return to the farm again tonight. I must see this wonder about which you tell me." Simeon stood up and lifted his arms toward heaven. "If this thing is true, then indeed 'I will give thanks unto the Lord with my whole heart.'"

"It *is* true, Father," Nathan said again, earnestly. Then he put his father's horn to his mouth and blew the signal the men used to call each other.

Asa and Joseph came running at the sound of the horn. They were surprised when they heard Simeon was going home with Nathan. They were even more surprised when told about Enoch. Joseph, who was a young man hardly more than a boy, looked at Nathan as though he would accuse him of playing a trick on his father. Asa was older. He was not so very old in years, but hard work had bent his shoulders. Nathan thought his eyes, under their bushy eyebrows, looked as though they had seen many things which were stored away in his head where he could look at them from the *back* of his eyes. There were times when Asa did not appear to be seeing you at all, even though his eyes were open. Nathan was sure that his sight was turned inward at those times. He had mentioned this once to Renah

but she said that she never had heard such a silly idea.

Asa was a gentle soul and Nathan loved him. He rejoiced with Simeon and Nathan over what had happened and said nothing about not believing. As they ate the food Anna had sent, Joseph began to question Nathan eagerly. "Was this Jesus a man great in size and strength? Did he look like a man who could lead a rebellion against the Roman rulers of Galilee?"

"Do not vex the lad with such questions," said Asa quietly. "This man is a teacher and a healer."

"Teachers have stirred up the people before," said Joseph, "and I have heard of the crowds that gather to hear him."

"I remember Judas of Galilee, and thousands of other Galileans who were put to death or sent away as slaves by the Roman general when I was a boy," said Simeon sternly, "so speak no more of rebellions."

Nathan was glad his father and Asa had stopped Joseph from asking him these questions which he did not know how to answer. He threw some crumbs to a little flock of goldfinches and linnets which were pecking at the stray kernels of wheat left on the ground. Jesus had said God cared what became of one little bird! Jesus had not talked about Rome. Nathan felt he would not care much about Rome. He would care more about God. For a few moments he did not hear what the men were saying, then he listened again, for Asa was speaking.

"What do we need more than we have?" Asa was saying. "Is not this pleasant land ours? Planting of seed and the harvest; work, and a quiet rest under the stars; are they not enough? Would the crops be better or the flowers brighter if the soil were mixed with blood?" Nathan followed Asa's gaze to where it appeared to rest on the snowy crown of Mount Hermon, far in the distance, and it seemed to Nathan as though Asa were looking at God. He spoke softly:

> " 'He causeth grass to grow for the cattle,
>   And herb for the service of man
>   That he may bring forth food out of the earth.
>
>   O Lord how manifold are thy works!
>   In wisdom hast thou made them all:
>   The earth is full of thy riches.' "

Joseph was grumbling. "You are old," he said to Asa, "and cannot understand the hopes of young men who want to free our people from Roman rulers. It is enough for you to sit and dream when your work in the fields is done."

Simeon laid his hand on Joseph's shoulder. "God is not served by hating," he said. Then he, too, looked out over his fields and the grain already harvested and stored in little sheds, as he added: "The riches of the earth are a goodly heritage."

Nathan turned from Joseph's angry frown to look at the smooth brow of Asa, and something he had heard Jesus say popped into his mind. It was when he had been talking about happiness, Nathan remembered. Jesus had said: "Happy are the gentle, for they will be heirs of the earth." That was like Asa, content with the riches of the earth. It was all he wanted, and there it was, ready for him to take.

Nathan, Boy of Capernaum

"Come, Nathan," said his father, jumping to his feet, "let us go home now."

As they walked back to the city, Nathan told his father of all that had happened the day before. It was good to walk and talk with his father. Nathan looked up with pride at the strong farmer with his dark skin and curly brown hair, and Simeon's eyes rested with tenderness on his young son. Nathan thought his father's eyes must have caught the blue of the sky from watching it for the sunshine or showers his crops needed. The wind, too, had blown through his hair and beard until it curled in all sorts of funny ways.

Simeon listened to Nathan's story. "A strange man indeed," he said thoughtfully, when Nathan had finished. "And you followed the crowd to the hills to see him, Nathan? And stood by his knee as you listened? A rabbi does not usually want a lap full of children when he is teaching. And then today he went home with you and sat down with your mother, a poor farmer's wife, while he gladdened her heart by healing her son. A proud man would have chosen to sit at meat with the rulers of the synagogue or some of our rich merchants. This man has fishermen for his friends and talks of happiness for the poor. I cannot understand who he is, but I know he has brought gladness to my house and that I must seek him out to thank him. Did you say he is at Simon Peter's house, Nathan?"

"Yes, Father. He comes from Nazareth. He told us about his home this afternoon. He is a carpenter, and poor too, so he knows and loves lowly people."

"That I have heard, and that he has given up his trade to

preach about what he calls the Kingdom of Heaven. There must be something in his words that people want to hear, since they are following him in such great numbers. But I have never before heard any preaching about a Kingdom of Heaven."

"It has something to do with children, Father," said Nathan. "That was the reason Jesus would not let Peter and the others send us away. He said: 'It is of such as these that the Kingdom of Heaven is built.' I didn't know what he meant, Father. I thought a kingdom meant a king, in Jerusalem, who would chase away the Romans and bring again the glory of David and Solomon."

"It was not of such a kingdom he spoke, of that I am sure," said Simeon, "though what he meant when he talked about children I cannot say. If he brings happiness to humble folk and healing to the sick, he must have such wisdom from God."

"He called God our Father, and said He cared for us." Nathan looked up at Simeon as he added: "It made me understand better about loving God with all my heart, as the Shema says, because he is my Father — like you."

Simeon put his hand on Nathan's head. "It is a new thought," he said slowly, "but I have been told he speaks differently from our teachers in the synagogue."

By this time they had reached the city and Simeon was walking so fast in his eagerness to see Enoch that Nathan had to run to keep up with him. When they arrived at the house they found the courtyard filled with people. The neighbors had not been able to keep from telling others, so quite a crowd had gathered. Enoch was a little frightened by so much attention and was holding fast to his mother's skirt while he tried to hide behind her. But when he saw his father and Nathan he forgot about the rest of the people and ran toward them. Simeon caught him up in his strong arms, then he said to the neighbors: "When the harvesting is over, my friends, we shall have a feast of thanksgiving together for the healing of my son, but now I would ask of you that you give us this moment alone."

When the people had gone, Anna led the way to the roof top and they sat down together in quietness. The sun was dropping behind the hills and the city was in shadow beneath them, but the sky was still bright. Simeon put Enoch on his feet and felt of his legs and back. The flesh was hard and firm. Simeon could hardly believe it as Enoch went from one to the other, laughing at their cries of joy. Then Anna gathered him into her arms while they talked of the friend who had done this wonderful thing for them. There was such happiness in their hearts that the sky was darkening and the first stars peeping through, before Simeon could bear to leave and go back to his farm.

Nathan and Enoch were nearly asleep, but they opened their eyes when their father moved to get up. Simeon lifted Enoch into his arms again as he said:

"This is the Lord's doing;
It is marvellous in our eyes."

Then, as they all stood together, Simeon poured out his heart in thanksgiving to God for His goodness to them. Anna,

The Farm

Renah, and Nathan joined in those words from the Sacred Scrolls which they knew and loved:

> "Thou hast put gladness in my heart."
> "How precious is thy loving kindness, O God!"
> "We give thanks unto thee, O God; we give thanks."

When at last his father left them, Nathan felt sure he would not rest that night until he, too, had tried to find Jesus to thank him.

Chapter v

THE HARVEST

"Happy they who hunger and thirst for goodness"

THE hot summer was nearly over and fruits hung heavy on the trees and vines of Galilee. On the hills behind Capernaum the vineyards were full of juicy bunches of purple grapes. To reach them the paths led through orchards of olive trees, their rich harvest half-hidden under grayish green leaves. There were also groves of walnut trees, and many fig trees with their gray trunks and thick green leaves. Down by the lake, date palm trees dangled luscious clusters of dates under a crown of broad palm branches.

This was the third big harvest of the year and was the one Nathan loved best. The other two came in the spring,

The Harvest

first the barley, and, about a month later, the wheat harvest. It was great fun to go into the fields when the grain was ripe and see the tall stalks bend and ripple in the breeze, while the air was sweet with the promise of bread. It was fun, too, when he could help in gathering the grain after it had been cut down, or in winnowing and sifting after the threshing. But the fruit harvest of late summer and early autumn was still more exciting. It seemed to Nathan that the ripe fruits held all the golden magic of the summer sun and the mystery of hidden streams deep down in the earth where only the roots of trees and vines could find them. It never rained in the summer, and yet in the fall the fruits were heavy with juice. Nathan could imagine how busily the roots must have twisted and bored to find those unseen springs and then carry their moisture back to the thirsty buds, making them swell into perfect figs or dates or grapes.

All the harvests were followed by holidays. The Jewish people called their holidays feast days. These feast days celebrated either a special event in their history or were days of rejoicing and thanksgiving for the harvests. Sometimes they celebrated both together and the festivities lasted a week. After the barley and wheat harvests came the Feast of Pentecost which lasted only one day but was very important. Thanks for the crops were given to God in the synagogues and at the great Temple at Jerusalem by an offering of the first two loaves of bread to be made from the new wheat. At the end of the day, when the festival meal was eaten in their homes, people invited the poor, or strangers, or other guests to share it with them. The Feast of Pentecost had been a time of great rejoicing in Nathan's family this year, not only for the harvest but because of the happiness that had come to them in the healing of little Enoch.

It had been a happy summer for them all. Now that his fields were bare and baked hard by the hot sun, Nathan's father was home with his family. Not until after the autumn rains could the farm be prepared and ploughed for another planting. Simeon now had work to do in his vineyards. The vines had to be watched so that insects would not destroy them, and sometimes it was necessary to cut away branches that were too heavy for the tender new growth. But he did not have to keep watch at night, until the fruit was ripe and ready to be picked. Simeon often went down to the shore and fished with the fishermen. Nathan and Enoch loved to go with him. They would follow their father out into the water until it was up to their knees. Simeon would go still farther, into deeper water which would be too deep for them. Whirling his net above his head, he would throw it out over the water, keeping the string which was fastened to the center of the net in his left hand. The weights around the edges would drag the net down beneath the water where it would trap any fish unlucky enough to be there. Then Simeon would jerk the string and the net would close like a bag as it was pulled in. Nathan and Enoch would jump and splash in glee if the catch was a good one, although they had to keep quiet while the fishing was going on.

Once or twice Simon Peter and Andrew had taken Nathan and Peter's son, Juda, a boy about Nathan's age, out in the boat with them. They left while the stars were

The Harvest

still shining and let down their nets in deep water far from shore. When the dawn came, the nets, heavy with fish, were hauled up and the fish emptied into the boat. A good catch meant money, for they were to be taken to the market place and sold. But Peter and Andrew had not done much fishing during the summer. They had been with Jesus of Nazareth who was preaching and teaching in the towns around the lake. They had even gone with him to his home town of Nazareth, in the hill country. No one knew when they would come or go, but Peter's house, near the shore, always had a crowd around the door if it were known that Jesus was in Capernaum.

Ever since the night when Simeon had gone to look for Jesus, that he might thank him for healing Enoch, he had been one of his friends. Nathan never knew whether his father had talked with Jesus in Peter's house or whether he had found him out under the stars near his own farm. But all through the summer Simeon had been among those who followed Jesus to listen to his teaching, or who gathered together to talk about the things he had said. Often they would meet on the roof top of Simeon's house and Nathan would slip quietly among them to listen until his eyes were heavy with sleep and he could hear no more.

One lovely day Simeon said to Anna: "Come, let us go around the shore, beyond the city, and take the children with us. The Master has gone in the boat with Peter and John to a cove where people can sit on the shore and hear him talk. We can spend the day there."

How joyfully they had hurried off, and, as they reached

67

the outskirts of the city, many other groups joined them. When they came to the hillside above a little bay, shaped like a horseshoe, they could see the boat drawing in toward the shore. People were scrambling down through the fields to meet it. But Jesus did not get out of the boat. He had Peter and John bring it into shallow water where it rocked gently as he spoke. Then he asked everyone to sit down. The shore sloped up so sharply around the cove that even those sitting at the top of the hill could hear what he said. Simeon and Anna managed to get close enough to the shore's edge for Nathan and Enoch to sit on a rock and dangle their feet in the cool water.

Then Jesus told stories which even children could understand. He talked about the planting of seed, and of the harvest which had just been gathered into the barns. He seemed to know how all these things were done. Simeon listened carefully and nodded his head from time to time to show that Jesus understood farming as well as he did himself. Jesus spoke of things that women knew about, too. He told of making bread, and now it was Anna who nodded and smiled. "The Kingdom of Heaven," said Jesus, "is like yeast which a woman takes and mixes with the flour so that the whole lump of dough may become light." Nathan had seen his mother do this nearly every day for her hungry family. He wondered what Jesus meant by saying that the Kingdom of Heaven was like yeast. Bread was not good without yeast. Perhaps people were not good without the Kingdom of Heaven. Perhaps the Kingdom of Heaven was goodness working in people. Even though one could not

68

The Harvest

always understand, still it was wonderful to listen to the stories Jesus told, Nathan thought, wriggling his toes in the blue water, while the prow of the boat in which Jesus sat scratched gently on the pebbles of the beach.

After awhile Peter and John turned the boat toward home, and the crowd began to go back to Capernaum or other towns from which they had come. Simeon took Enoch in his arms part of the way, for it was a long walk, and Nathan ran along with children of his own age who had come with their parents. The older people walked and talked together. Nathan would never forget that day.

Now the end of summer had come, and early autumn brought with it the festival of thanksgiving for the fruits of the tree and vine. There would be a whole week of joy and worship, in which everyone lived out-of-doors in little houses made from the branches of trees. This was called the Feast of Tabernacles. A tabernacle meant a kind of shelter such as a tent, hut, or booth. The Feast of Tabernacles was held not only to celebrate the fruit harvest, but to remind the Jewish people of the time when their ancestors, the Israelites, lived in tents while Moses was leading them out of Egypt, across the wilderness, to the Promised Land. Many people went from Capernaum to Jerusalem to keep this feast by giving thanks to God in the great Temple there. Others built their booths on the roof tops at home or in the fields outside the city. Here they lived for a week, going to the synagogue each day to join in the service which the Sacred Law required of them at this season.

Simeon took his family out to the hills with many of

their neighbors who also had vineyards or worked in vineyards belonging to someone else. Asa and Joseph, who had helped with the barley and wheat harvests, were there with their families. Nathan ran out joyfully with the other children to help the men by gathering the branches which they had cut from the trees, and from which they would build the booths. When the men had finished, the hillside looked like a great arbor or bower.

Every man, woman, and child had a share in gathering the fruit. While men and women stripped the vines, the children put the grapes in baskets and carried them to the wine presses where the juice was squeezed out and poured into large stone jars. But before keeping any of the fruit for their own use, the very finest grapes were taken to the synagogue for an offering to God. This was done with the olives, too, and with every kind of fruit. The Jewish people believed that the best of everything belonged to God, and they never failed at any of their feasts to put the first share on the altar where they worshiped.

Nathan worked hard with the grapes. He could carry quite a large basket on his shoulder. He had not yet learned to balance carefully enough to carry it on his head, but Renah could carry hers on her head as easily as Anna did. Even Enoch had his basket and worked along happily. Nathan loved to see the purple juice pour out of the vats where the grapes were crushed. It made him thirsty for the sharp, sweet taste and he sucked at his stained fingers. Enoch copied him and pretty soon they were laughing at each other because their lips as well as their fingers were purple.

The Harvest

Then there were the olive trees. Men and boys climbed up and shook the branches, sending a shower of olives to the ground. Sometimes they used long poles to knock down those which still clung to the branches. Women and children would gather basketfuls and carry them to the olive mills where they were to be crushed and their oil collected in jars.

Figs and dates were picked from the trees, and many were spread out on roof tops or in sunny places to dry for winter food. So the harvesting of the fruits was just as busy a time as the season of the grain harvests. It was even more fun for the children, because everyone was living out-of-doors and it seemed like a big picnic. At night, under the leafy roofs of their booths, they sang songs of thanksgiving while the light of moon and stars filtered in and made silvery patterns on the ground. Nathan thought the sound of so many voices thanking Him must be pleasing to God.

"O praise the Lord, all ye nations:
Praise him all ye people.
For his merciful kindness is great toward us:
And the truth of the Lord endureth for ever.
Praise ye the Lord."

The deep tones of the men and the higher soft, sweet voices of the women echoed back and forth from booth to booth until the whole hillside seemed to be ringing. There were the voices of the children, too, like the little pipes made of reeds that they used in their games. And, over all, the rustle of the wind in the leafy walls and covering of the booths, making a music of its own.

71

Nathan, Boy of Capernaum

When the singing was over, Nathan begged his father for a story about Moses and the Israelites, and of how they lived in tents on their long journey from Egypt to the new home God had promised them. So Simeon told about that city of tents which moved from place to place in the desert, and he described the big tent, called the Tabernacle, which was made for the worship of God. "It was a place of meeting for all the people," said Simeon, "and it was made of the most beautiful and costly gifts they had to offer. God told Moses just how this Tabernacle should be made. It must have ten curtains of violet, purple, and scarlet linen, hung from poles of acacia wood, with goat skins on top to keep out the rain. Inside, all the gifts of gold, silver, bronze, and precious stones were to be used for decoration so that this place of meeting might be as beautiful and holy as they could make it, because God would meet there with them. But the most important place in the Tabernacle was kept for the Ark of the Covenant, a box which held the Ten Commandments which God had given to Moses on Mount Sinai. If the people obeyed these laws, God had promised Moses that He would lead them safely to the land of Canaan."

"The Ark was made of acacia wood and covered with gold," cried Nathan.

"And had rings at both ends with poles through them, so it could be carried on the shoulders of the men when the Israelites moved from one place to another," added Renah.

"Yes," said Simeon, "the people of Israel carried their place of worship with them until they reached the end of their traveling and came to the land where they could settle down and build a temple of stone for the worship of God."

"They were a long time in the wilderness, weren't they, Father?" asked Nathan.

"Forty years," answered Simeon. "Boys like you grew up to be men with families of their own, and the older men and women died and were buried in the desert without ever seeing the new land."

"Why did it take so long?" Enoch lifted his curly head from his mother's lap and looked up at her in surprise.

"Because," said Anna quietly, "most of the people were afraid to do as God wanted them to do. They thought the people of Canaan were stronger than they and would do them harm. They forgot that God was taking care of them."

"So, because some were timid and would not trust God," Simeon went on, "all the Israelites had to wander about in the desert for forty years before God thought they were ready to go into the beautiful land He had promised them. The men and women who had refused to go at first were dead by this time, and others, who were brave and strong, had taken their places as leaders under Moses. So God gave them another chance. He led them to the shore of the river Jordan and showed them again the beautiful land of Canaan on the other side. Then God took Moses to live with Him, for Moses was now a very old man and tired from the long years of traveling about. And God chose Joshua to lead his people across the river into the Promised Land. When Joshua gave the command to go forward, the Ark of the Covenant, carried on the shoulders of four holy men, went first and all the great company of the Israelites followed after. So all who trusted God's promise came to the new country."

Nathan tried to imagine what it would be like to pack up your home, and even the place where you worshiped God, and move from place to place without getting anywhere. And all the time there was a lovely land, such as this land of Galilee, waiting for the wanderers if they only would have courage and trust in God to reach it. It always gave Nathan a start of surprise to remember that Galilee was really a part of that land of Canaan into which his people had finally come so many years ago.

"I'm sure," he said aloud, "that the people of Israel were very glad to get at last to a land where there was milk and honey and fruit, and where they could build themselves houses instead of tents. They must have been tired of the wilderness."

"It was not God's will that they should stay so long in the wilderness," said Renah. "That was *their own* will."

Nathan remembered Jesus had said something like that when he was asking him about Enoch's fall. Jesus had said that God wanted people to be happy. That when they were hurt or unhappy it was not God's will, but because they had followed *their own* will.

Renah went on: "They had to work hard for their food in the new land, and it was a long time before they could settle down and enjoy themselves."

Nathan looked out through the open side of the booth at the vineyards covering the slope of the hill. The moon

was like a tipped basin spilling a silver shower over the earth. It made the leaves of the olive trees shine like polished metal, and bathed the leafy booths in a silvery flood. Nathan was thinking proudly now of his forefathers who had followed Joshua across the river Jordan to take this land — this very land of his — as their own. God had given them success and had raised up great men and prophets in Israel. The stories were in the Sacred Scrolls. Then there had been kings like Saul and David and Solomon. But that was a long time ago.

Now Rome ruled nearly the whole world and many people did not like the Romans. They talked among themselves about the coming of a new leader who should restore the kingdom of Israel. Joseph and many other young men met together secretly. Nathan had heard his mother and father talk about it. They wanted to make Jesus a king. Nathan's heart swelled as he imagined what a wonderful king Jesus would be. But he didn't seem to want to be that kind of king. The kingdom he talked about was different. It was like seed planted in the earth, or like yeast in a bowl of flour. It was a kind of goodness. Nathan wrinkled his forehead. Was that what Jesus had meant when he said: "Happy are they who hunger and thirst for goodness"?

Anna leaned forward and put out her hand to brush back the hair which had fallen over Nathan's eyes. "What are you thinking about, little son?" she asked.

"About being hungry and thirsty," answered Nathan.

"Dear me," said his mother in surprise, "we finished our evening meal just a short time ago."

"But I mean something else," said Nathan slowly, wondering how he could put it into words, "I mean being hungry and thirsty for goodness. Is goodness a kind of food, Mother?"

"He says the strangest things, Mother," said Renah. "What are you talking about, Nathan?"

"I know what he means," said Anna, "and it is not strange at all, since there are many ways of being hungry and thirsty. There is hunger and thirst for food and drink. The body needs them in order to live, so we feel an appetite which is satisfied by eating and drinking. That is why we work hard in the fields and on the sea to provide for these needs of the body. Then there is the hunger for riches, or for pleasure, and sometimes an appetite for things that are bad for you. But there is also inside us something which wants a different kind of food than any of these. I think Nathan meant this when he asked if goodness was a kind of food. We are hungry and thirsty for goodness when we want to do right more than anything else. And we are not satisfied until we have done it. Did you hear Jesus speak of this, Nathan?"

"Yes, when he was talking on the hillside that first day, Mother. He said: 'Happy are they who hunger and thirst for goodness, for they will be satisfied.'" Nathan remembered the faces of the crowd as Jesus was speaking. Yes, that was it, they were hungry faces. But not for bread. They wanted something more than bread. Nathan had seen the faces change as they listened to Jesus. He was giving them food which satisfied that kind of hunger and thirst.

Simeon got up and pushed back one of the branches which had broken loose and hung across the wide entrance to their booth. "Look," he said, "out there is the good land which God gave to our forefathers when they were worthy to take it. They planted seed and raised crops, as has been done to this day. Our people have eaten of the fruit of the tree and vine, and have satisfied their thirst with water and milk and the juice of the grape. There has been plenty and Israel has been a great nation." Simeon's eyes looked beyond his vineyards to the far-distant hills, and the eyes of his wife and children followed his gaze. After a moment Simeon spoke again: "But now I believe there is a new country for our people to enter, and God has sent a leader, as He sent Moses to the Israelites of old."

"Do you mean Jesus, Father?" cried Nathan.

"Yes," answered his father. "And all who are hungry and thirsty for goodness will follow him. But those who want riches and selfish pleasures, or who are afraid, will stay outside as the Israelites stayed in the desert."

"Father," asked Nathan eagerly, "will it be the kingdom of heaven?"

"It will be the Kingdom of Heaven, little Nathan, a kingdom we shall feel and not see, for its roots are in our hearts and its fruit is love."

Chapter vi

THE SHEPHERD

"Happy the merciful"

SIMEON had a younger brother who was a shepherd. His name was Benjamin and his home was in Magdala, a few miles from Capernaum, but most of the time Benjamin was taking care of his sheep on the hills or in the green valleys of the beautiful countryside that stretched beyond the town. He not only watched his own flock, but took care of his neighbors' flocks as well. Sometimes shepherds did this for people who had other work to do.

Nathan loved to go out on the hills with the sheep, so one morning when his father asked him to take a message to his Uncle Benjamin, Nathan got ready very happily for the trip.

"Would you like to see if Juda, the son of Simon Peter, can go with you"? asked Simeon. "It is too far for Enoch, and I think you might like to have another boy for company."

Anna looked up from her work. "I do not know whether his mother can spare him," she said. "Peter is still away and Juda is a great help at home. But run and find out, Nathan. I would rather have two of you go together."

It did not take many minutes for Nathan to run down to the shore. He found Juda in front of his house helping to make butter by beating a goat-skin bag which had been partly filled with milk. It took a good deal of shaking and beating to churn the milk into butter, sometimes half a day, so Nathan's face fell. He was afraid Juda's mother would not be able to let him go before his task was completed. But, when Juda heard what Nathan had come for, he ran to beg his mother to let him off.

Peter's wife, Sara, came to the door to ask Nathan how long they would be gone. She was smiling so Nathan's hopes rose. "My father says we may spend the night with my uncle and come back tomorrow," he answered. "Do let Juda go with me."

"Well, then," said Sara, making her words come very slowly because she could see that their feet were fairly dancing with excitement, "I guess I shall have to let him go."

Nathan and Juda shouted with joy and Sara's mother came to the door to see what all the noise was about. When Sara told her of the trip the boys were taking, she said she would prepare a good lunch for them to carry with them. While they were waiting, Sara gave Nathan a message for his mother and father. "Tell them," she said, "I had a traveler here last night who brought me news of Simon Peter and Andrew. They are doing very many wonderful things as they carry the Good News of the kingdom for the Master."

Nathan knew that Jesus had sent twelve of his closest friends to travel through Galilee teaching and healing. He had trained them for this work. Jesus, himself, had taken another road into the nearby towns alone. Anna and Simeon had talked about it and wondered whether Peter and Andrew, who had gone together, would be able to do this work which was so different from their trade as fishermen. They would be glad to hear this news of them for it was now several months since Peter and Andrew and the others had started out. Nathan wondered if Sara had word, also, of Jesus. But when he asked her she shook her head.

"The traveler came from another direction," Sara said, "and I have no way of hearing until the day the Master enters Capernaum again. Maybe, Nathan," she added eagerly, "you and Juda might hear some word of him up Magdala way."

This thought made Nathan in a hurry to be off, and he was glad when Juda came running out of the house with his little bag of lunch slung over his shoulder. They had to go back to Nathan's house first, but it did not take long to get Simeon's message for his brother, Benjamin, and the basket of food which Anna had already packed.

"We shall have plenty to eat," laughed Juda, showing his own bag.

"You can share with Benjamin and the little shepherd boy who helps him, if you have too much," said Anna with a smile. "I put in some extra for them anyway," she added, for she knew the appetite of ten-year-old boys and wanted them to feel they could eat all they cared to.

So Nathan and Juda scampered off in great good humor. Over their short robes they wore an outer coat, called an aba, which they could wrap around them when they slept on the ground as the shepherds did. It was a bright morning, just before the heavy autumn rains set in, and the boys felt they were lucky to be outside with the blue sky above their heads, instead of in the synagogue school under the sharp eye of the rabbi. As they raced along the road, which followed the shore of the lake, they skirted many little coves and bays where fishing boats rocked in the shallow water while fishermen mended their nets. This made the way longer than if they had been able to go in a straight line, but it was fun to stop a moment in these fishing villages and watch the men at their work. In one village, Bethsaida,

The Shepherd

Nathan and Juda saw Zebedee, the father of James and John, working on the beach, while their mother Salome spun her yarn in the doorway of their home. Nathan loved these two brothers, particularly John, because he was so straight and strong and swift in all he did. Nathan thought he would like to grow to be like John and spend his life working for Jesus. James and John had gone out with the other friends whom Jesus had sent to teach and heal. Their mother's eyes seemed to be watching for them as she worked on her wool.

Once in a while Nathan and Juda stopped to bathe their dusty feet in the cool water, or take it up in their hands to splash over their faces and necks. It was not very long until they came to the town of Magdala, for it was only a few miles from Capernaum. It was a pretty city on the shore of the lake, and close to a green and fruitful part of the country known as the Plain of Gennesaret. Sometimes the Sea of Galilee was called the Lake of Gennesaret.

The people of Magdala had a trade which we would think strange today. In a ravine with high rocky sides, not far from the town, thousands of doves or pigeons built their nests. Boys and men would snare or trap these birds and sell them to dealers in Jerusalem. These men sold them again to people who wanted to buy an offering to place on the altar of the Great Temple. They had been taught that God would be pleased with such sacrifices. Poor people could buy a dove when they could not buy a larger animal.

Nathan and Juda passed men with baskets full of doves hung across the backs of donkeys on which they were traveling to Jerusalem. Nathan felt sorry for the poor frightened birds. He wondered if God would not rather have them free in the air where they belonged. He was sure Jesus would think so, because he had said God cared for birds.

In the low hills beyond the town, Nathan and Juda found Benjamin. All around on the grassy plains, and in the little valleys, sheep were grazing. Benjamin was glad to see Nathan and he gave a warm welcome to Juda. At the sound of their voices a shepherd boy, whose name was Neri, came running to see who it was that had arrived. He gave them a shy greeting. Benjamin asked them to sit down on the grass while Nathan delivered Simeon's message. As it was near the middle of the day and the sun was still hot, even though the summer was over, the boys sat in the shade of a big walnut tree and talked with Neri, who was delighted to have some boys of his own age to talk to. He showed them the slingshot which he carried to scare off any beasts which might try to hurt the sheep. He explained that the most dangerous animals slipped in among the sheep when it was dark. This gave Nathan and Juda a creepy feeling and made them wish they had brought slingshots of their own.

Benjamin invited the boys to share the lunch which he carried in a small bag fastened to his belt. But Nathan and Juda opened the bags of food they had brought with them and showed the extra share that Anna had packed for Benjamin and his helper. This made Neri's eyes shine, and Benjamin too was pleased.

It was a happy day. Just to wander through the fields

where the flocks of sheep were pastured was joy enough. Benjamin said Nathan and Juda might lead some of the sheep down to the well for water. He told them how to call the sheep, and the boys did their best. But the sheep were confused and ran one way and then another, but never in the direction the boys wanted them to. Then Benjamin laughed and called several of the leaders of the flock by name. Now the sheep knew the voice of their shepherd, and all turned and trotted after him as Benjamin led the way. Neri drew the water out of the well in a bucket and poured it into a trough for the sheep to drink. Then Nathan and Juda took turns drawing it.

When the afternoon was nearly over, and the shadows were reaching longer and longer across the fields, Benjamin and Neri began to call their flocks together. They must be put in a safe place for the night. Part way back, toward the city, was the sheepfold where the sheep were put at night during the spring, summer, and autumn months. It had no roof, such as the winter fold had, but there were strong walls of stone to keep the sheep from getting out and to protect them from wild beasts or robbers. There was only one opening through which the sheep could go into the fold. After they were all in, Benjamin, like other shepherds, would lie down in front of this little door to see that nothing got inside to harm them.

Nathan watched the woolly, gray-white bodies of the sheep push against each other in their eagerness to answer the shepherd's call, and soon they were all bunched together in one great mass to follow after Benjamin and Neri. Nathan

85

and Juda ran along with them and chased those sheep which had wandered off to nibble at an extra juicy root, back with the rest of the flock.

It was not until all were in the fold that Benjamin missed one of the lambs. Nathan did not see how he could tell, when he had so many, that one little lamb was not there. But Benjamin was sure, and said he must make haste to find it as it would be dark very soon. Nathan wanted to go with him, so they left Neri and Juda to sit by the door of the fold while they set out on their search. Benjamin kept calling and, after a while, he stopped. "Do you hear anything?" he asked Nathan.

Nathan thought he had heard a little cry but it was so faint he couldn't be sure, so Benjamin called once more. Now they could hear a bleating from the direction of some thorn bushes. As they got nearer they caught a gleam of white. Nathan started to run toward it but his uncle stopped him. "You would frighten the little animal," he said. "He may be caught on the sharp thorns and would tear his flesh if he struggled." So they went up to the bushes very quietly and Benjamin found it had happened just as he had thought. The lamb was caught in a thicket of thorns and could not free himself. Very gently Benjamin pulled the branches back and lifted the little creature out.

"Well, well, my wee one," scolded Benjamin gently, "it would have been better if you had not left your mother's side. But lambs are like children," and his eyes twinkled as he looked at Nathan. "They run away and always get into trouble. The jackals and wolves would have had a tender meal tonight if we had not found you." Then Benjamin tore a strip of cloth from his robe and bound up the bleeding leg. When he had finished, he took the lamb in his arms and held it against his breast in the folds of his coat. "Now," he said, "we will get back to the fold."

Nathan noticed how gladly and comfortably the lamb cuddled down in Benjamin's arms. He thought it must have felt the kind heart which beat beneath it. And Benjamin's face was happy with the joy of having found this smallest one of his flock. Faces are always happy when they are kind, thought Nathan. Then he remembered, as he always did when he thought of happiness, the day Jesus had talked about it on the hillside. Nathan had discovered many things since that day. Now he was seeing what Jesus meant when he said: "Happy are the merciful," for mercy was kindness.

Juda and Neri were glad, too, when they saw that the lamb had been found, and the mother sheep was gladdest of all. In the night, when the cry of a wolf or other animal sounded all too close, Nathan drew his cloak around him more tightly and felt happy that no sharp teeth could tear the flesh of these helpless creatures in the sheepfold while their kind shepherd, Benjamin, was taking care of them. Once Benjamin stood up and Nathan heard the hum of his sling. The shadowy shapes which had been drawing near disappeared in the darkness.

In the morning Nathan and Juda had to say goodbye to Benjamin and Neri for they had been told to come home early. As they went back through Magdala, they saw a crowd gathering in one of the streets. It was a street in which many of the wealthier people of the town had their homes, and it was at the entrance to the courtyard of one of these homes that the crowd seemed thickest. Nathan started to run. "Come on, Juda," he called over his shoulder, "it may be Jesus of Nazareth."

"I don't think so," Juda said as he followed. "That is probably the house of a rich Pharisee and they don't like Jesus very well."

Nathan thought Juda was right about this, but he wanted to see what was going on anyway. So the boys elbowed their way between the older people in the crowd until they reached a place where they could see into the courtyard. The dining room of the house opened upon this courtyard and they could see men seated around the table. "Whose house is this?" Nathan heard someone ask of another person.

"It belongs to Simon, the Pharisee," was the answer. "He is entertaining the new teacher and healer at dinner. I would like to hear what they are saying."

Nathan's heart thumped hard. Yes, there was Jesus at the table. Nathan longed to run across the courtyard and curl up at his feet. Juda, too, was breathing hard with excitement at the sight of the Master whom they all loved, and for whom his father had gone to preach and teach the Good News of the Kingdom. But, almost at the moment they recognized Jesus, a woman slipped out of the crowd and swiftly crossed the courtyard to the table where the company was eating and drinking. She was neither a rich nor a proud woman, for her hair hung long over her shoulders and she wore only a plain robe clasped tightly about her.

The Shepherd

She stopped before Jesus and bowed her head. Nathan could see that she was crying. It was all so sudden that no one said a word until the woman fell to her knees and opened a little bottle of spiced oil and poured it out on Jesus's feet. This was the custom for an honored guest before dining, but Simon had not thought Jesus was important enough for this honor and had not done it.

Nathan heard gasps of surprise in the crowd. Then someone said: "The teacher must know that the woman is wicked. She is not fit to go near him." Simon, the host, also was looking angry and was saying something to Jesus about the woman. But Jesus's face was not troubled. He was looking at the woman, Nathan thought, just as Benjamin had looked at the hurt lamb — so kind, so full of mercy. Then Jesus turned his head toward Simon, and Nathan couldn't hear what he said, but he seemed to be telling a story. Simon was listening with a frown to what Jesus was saying. After a few moments Jesus turned back to the woman with a smile. Her face was raised to his, and Nathan heard only one word of what Jesus said to her — the word "forgive." But as she came back through the courtyard and disappeared into the crowd, the woman's face had that light which Nathan had seen shining on other faces, although her cheeks were still wet with tears.

After this interruption to his dinner, Simon sent servants to close the door of his courtyard and to order the crowd away from his house. So Nathan and Juda squeezed through the crowd again and soon were running along the shore road which led back to Capernaum. They were excited to think they had news of Jesus for their families and friends, and were happy to know he was so near home. Perhaps in a few days he would be back among the people who loved him so dearly. Perhaps, too, Peter and Andrew, James and John, and all the others who had been away, would be meeting him there in Capernaum.

"Nathan," said Juda, after they had gone a little way, "that woman was kinder to Jesus than anyone in the house. She poured her spiced oil on his feet, and it costs a great deal of money. I don't believe she was wicked. Anyhow, she loved him very much."

"Well," said Nathan, remembering the woman's face, "She wasn't happy when she went there, but she was happy when she left. I guess her thought meant more to Jesus than her sin, so he was kind." Nathan thought again of the little lost lamb and Benjamin, the good shepherd. Perhaps Jesus was like that with people.

Chapter vii

THE POOL

"Happy the pure in heart"

THE first autumn rains were falling on Capernaum and all the land of Galilee. Nathan pulled his cloak around him as tightly as he could to keep himself dry as he ran back and forth to the synagogue school. The water in the street bubbled up between his toes, and he had to shake the drops which fell from his hair out of his eyes. He liked the feel of rain on his face. It made him think how good it must seem to the dry earth which was baked to a hard brown crust after the long summer. The hills beyond the city looked dark as the rain lashed at them and washed away the dust and dried leaves from the trees. It made the rocks stand out almost black. But somehow, thought Nathan, they all seemed more alive — like giants waking up refreshed from a long nap, and stretching and shaking themselves awake.

Out on his father's farm, Nathan knew the rain would strike deeper and deeper into the ground until it was all soft and spongy again. Then the oxen would be fastened to the plough once more and Simeon, or Asa, or Joseph would drive them up and down the broad fields, turning the earth in even furrows until it was ready for the sowing of a new crop of wheat, corn, and barley.

Back in the hills and through the valleys, streams, too, were filling up. They would grow into noisy brooks where there had been only a bare trickle of water before the rains started. Pools which had almost dried up would get deep and cool again. Nathan knew how to find these pools by following the sheep and goat tracks. He had gone in the early spring with some older boys to swim in the clear, cold water of one of them.

Down by the shore the winds at times whipped the waves of the lake to twice their usual height. Then they pounded against docks and fish wharves with great fury. Or, when the wind died and the waters of the lake were quiet, the rain made a mist like smoke rising from its surface. Boats were beached until the storms were over. There was something clean about the rain, even on the seashore where there was always plenty of water, thought Nathan. The wharves, where the fishermen sorted and cleaned their fish, did not smell so strong after they had been washed by torrents of

The Pool

rain water, and the boats looked as though they had been freshly painted.

There was no living on the roof tops these days, but it was cosy in the house. Anna did her baking in a large oven which kept the house warm and gave out pleasant odors when Nathan came in from school wet and often chilly. The days were growing shorter now, so, when her family gathered from work or play at the evening hour, Anna took oil and filled a little lamp made of clay. Then she lighted the wick and placed it where it would give most light to all in the house.

On special occasions there were also candles to be lighted. In the middle of winter, for instance, there would be the Feast of Lights. At this time a candle would be lighted for every member of the family, and on each of the eight days of the Feast a new candle would be added for everyone until the house was blazing with light. The whole city would be full of light, for the Feast of Lights was a season of great rejoicing. One hundred and fifty years before Nathan's day, the Temple at Jerusalem had been given back to the Jewish people after it had been for a long time in the hands of their enemies. One of their great national heroes, Judas Maccabeus, had done this wonderful deed. People called it the cleansing or purifying of the Temple, and the celebration of this event was a very happy time. Nathan had never seen the Temple. Boys who lived a long way from Jerusalem were not usually taken up to the feasts until they were twelve years old. But every Jewish boy was taught to think of the Temple, as their ancestors, the Israelites, had thought of their

Nathan, Boy of Capernaum

Tabernacle, or tent of worship, as the place where God was closest to His people. And there was not a boy who did not know the stories of its glorious history.

So the rainy season and the winter were not dull for Nathan. The Sea of Galilee was low, like water in the bottom of a bowl. Its shores were protected on all sides by a circle of hills. The harsh, cold winds, which swept the higher and more mountainous parts of the country, did not affect the climate of towns like Capernaum, or Bethsaida, or Magdala. After the rains were over there would be many days of bright sunshine and mild temperatures all winter, even though the crown of snow on Mount Hermon in the distance grew heavier and heavier.

On an afternoon, while the rain was still falling, Nathan lingered in the market place on his way home from school. He sniffed the keen, wet air and drew it deep into his lungs until he felt clean inside. Then he looked around to see if any caravans had arrived. It was always fun to get near enough to hear what these travelers from far countries were talking about. They brought news as well as goods with them. Today, most of the shopkeepers of the market place had moved their wares back under cover because of the rain, but Nathan was quick to discover a group of wet camels and donkeys huddled together in front of one of these shops. The front was open so it was easy to look inside. Nathan ran over and stood with other boys who wanted to see what was going on. There were, also, older men and women who had stopped to look and listen.

The merchants, who were seated on mats inside the shop,

The Pool

Nathan could see were from the South. They were **Arabs** who had traveled from the desert plains of Arabia, perhaps all the way from Egypt. They seemed to have important news and their faces were dark with anger. There were several merchants of his own people, too. Nathan thought they must have come in company with the Arabs up the Jordan valley from Jericho or Jerusalem. They were all so intent on their conversation that they paid no heed to the people who were standing around to listen.

Just inside the open doorway stood a man whom **Nathan** knew. He was an important leader of the synagogue. His name was Jairus and his daughter was a friend of Nathan's sister, Renah. Jairus was a loyal and devoted friend of Jesus because Jesus had gone to his house and healed his daughter, Esther, when everyone thought she was dead. Simeon, Nathan's father, and Jairus were also good friends. Jairus was listening with a troubled face to what the merchants were saying. Nathan moved closer to him without being noticed. No one paid much attention to what children did in Capernaum unless they were in the way. Then they were chased off in short order, and not always very gently.

Nathan could not understand a great deal of what the men were saying. Their heads and beards wagged as their voices rumbled on. It was something about Herod, the ruler of Galilee. Well, Nathan had heard plenty of angry talk about Herod, even in *his* short life. The Jewish people hated him, and probably now there was a new reason for their ill feeling. Then Nathan heard them speak of John. Was it John the fisherman, the friend of Jesus, whom **Nathan**

The Pool

loved as though he were his older brother? Nathan listened with fear in his heart. No, it was John the Baptizer. Nathan knew about him, too. He was a holy man who had preached down at the river Jordan. Many people had followed him there, and he had scolded them for their wrongdoing. When they promised to change their ways and do right, John led them into the river where their sins were all washed away. He called this baptizing. Andrew and John had gone to hear John the Baptizer and had met Jesus there. What were the merchants saying? Herod had put John the Baptizer to death? Nathan looked up, horrified, at Jairus. Why, he wondered, would Herod kill this good man? Jairus folded his cloak more closely about him as though he were cold. He did not see Nathan, but his lips were moving and Nathan could just hear him as he said almost in a whisper: "It will not be safe for Jesus now. He must go away." Then Jairus turned and moved along the street toward the synagogue. Nathan, his heart beating hard, ran all the way home. It would be terrible, he felt, if Jesus had to go away and not return. He had not come back yet from this last trip, although Nathan and Juda had thought, after seeing him in Magdala, that it would be only a few days before he would be in Capernaum again.

When Nathan reached home he found there were guests. Peter's wife, Sara, and her mother were sitting with Anna, while Renah and Esther, Jairus's daughter, were stringing some beads as they listened to the older women talk. Juda was there, too, playing with Enoch.

Anna looked up in surprise when Nathan rushed in with

his cheeks flushed, and all out of breath. "What is the matter, my son?" she asked. "Did someone chase you? Or have you been in some mischief?"

"No, Mother," said Nathan. He could not say more until he had swallowed a few times to get rid of the lump in his throat which almost stopped his breathing. Juda and Enoch jumped up to tug at his wet cloak until it dropped to the floor in a little pool of water.

"Come then," said his mother, "and sit where it is warm and dry. Have you news, Nathan, that you come running in with no manners at all, not even a greeting for our guests?"

The women had stopped their work and were watching Nathan with fear in their faces, waiting for him to answer his mother's question. Perhaps something had happened to Peter or Andrew, or some of the others who had gone away.

"There are merchants here from the South," said Nathan at last. "I heard them talking in the shop of Ezra ben Levi in the market place."

"And what did they say?" Sara could hardly wait for him to go on.

"They said Herod had killed John the Baptizer. They were very angry, and all who listened were angry."

"John the Baptizer put to death? Ah, that is sad news indeed," cried Anna. "Herod had him in prison. Was not that enough? Who was there, Nathan, at the shop of Ezra ben Levi?"

"I saw Jairus," answered Nathan. "I heard him say it would not be safe for Jesus now. Do you think so, Mother? Will Jesus have to go away?"

The Pool

"How could anyone want to hurt Jesus?" asked Esther, dropping her beads. "What does my father mean?"

"He means that Jesus must go where Herod is not the ruler and has no power to harm the holy men of our people," answered Sara. "But," she added proudly, "that will be as Jesus wishes. Herod can have no power over him unless it is his will. Did the merchants say anything about the Master? Or of Peter and the rest?"

"They spoke of crowds — and a 'new leader.' I could not understand all they said, but I did not hear the names of Peter or Andrew or any of our friends. Do you think the 'new leader' is Jesus?"

"We shall know more about this when Simeon comes home," said Anna. "Now go and play with Juda and Enoch, Nathan, and do not fear for the Master. It will be as Sara has said. No one can harm Jesus unless it is his will."

Sara and her mother got up and said they had better go back to their home. This news might mean that Peter and Andrew would be coming soon. Jesus might want his friends to meet him here to talk over this dreadful thing that had happened. Juda had better come with them as there would be work for him to do.

Esther wanted to run home and hear from her father more about what had happened, so soon they had all gone. Anna put down her work and started to move about, making preparations for the evening meal. Nathan did not feel like playing. He wanted to know more about John the Baptizer. Renah had questions to ask, too. "Wasn't John a kinsman of Jesus?" she asked her mother.

"His mother and Mary of Nazareth, the mother of Jesus, were cousins," Anna told her.

"Why did John baptize people in the river, Mother?" asked Nathan. "Could he really make them good that way?"

"No, my Nathan," said Anna. "John did not baptize people until they had decided they wanted to stop doing wrong and begin doing what he told them was right. Their hearts had to change first. Then he led them into the water because water means cleanness. Baptism was a sign of washing away the old sin and making the heart all clean and pure again."

Nathan thought about this a few moments. He remembered one time, not very long ago, Benjamin had bought some sheep from another shepherd. Their backs had been marked with the mark of the shepherd who had sold them. Nathan had seen Benjamin take them to the water and wash off the old mark. Then he had put his own mark on the sheep to show that they now belonged to him. Perhaps when people were baptized by John, an old mark was washed off and a new one was put on them, like the sheep. Only the marks were inside instead of outside. He asked his mother about this.

"Yes, Nathan," Anna said, stopping with the warm loaves she had taken from the oven still in her hands, "I think it *is* like that. The marks are inside because they are in the heart. The old mark is the feeling which makes us want to do wrong things, and the new mark is the feeling which makes us want to do right. The old mark is hate, and greed, and selfishness. The new one is love and kindness."

The Pool

"But Mother," said Renah, "the new mark on a sheep means he belongs to a new shepherd. Did people who were baptized by John and had the new mark of love in their hearts belong to someone?"

"John thought they did," said Anna quietly. "He meant it to be a sign that they belonged to a new leader and were ready to follow him. Peter and John and many others have thought so, too."

"You mean Jesus, Mother?" asked Nathan.

"Yes, son," answered Anna with a smile.

Long after Nathan had curled up on his sleeping rug that night he could hear the sound of the rain in the courtyard, and the drip of water on the roof from the branches of the olive tree. It made him think again about things being made clean outside, and of how bright and fresh everything would look when the sun came out. Even the air would shine as though it had been washed. Then he thought of other kinds of cleanness. There was the washing of one's hands before eating, and there was the food itself which must be clean. Nathan was taught in the synagogue school that certain kinds of food were not right to eat. There were rules in the Books of the Law about what the Jewish people should be allowed to use as food. The children learned these rules by heart:

> "These are the beasts which ye shall eat:
> The ox, the sheep and the goat. . . .
>
> Of all clean birds shall ye eat.
> But these are they of which ye shall not eat. . . ."

Nathan, Boy of Capernaum

All the food that they were forbidden to eat was called unclean, but Nathan did not understand why. All he knew was that being clean seemed to be important in many different ways. And it must be both outside and inside. One day his mother had given him a cup to wash and dry. Nathan had polished it very carefully on the outside to make it look shiny, but Anna had said, "Don't forget the inside, Nathan. It is the inside of the cup that holds what we drink, so that must be clean, too."

The rain kept on drip — drip — drip, and Nathan was growing sleepy. He did not hear his father come home, or the sound of voices as Simeon and Anna talked together of the sad news which had been brought to Capernaum by the travelers from the South. Nathan was in a dream country, though it seemed very real to him.

He was running along a path in the hills. The air was sweet with the freshness that comes after rain, and the sky was bright above his head where the branches of the trees parted to let sunlight filter through. Soon he came to the little pool he had been looking for. It was at the foot of a big rock and Nathan got down on his hands and knees and leaned over it so he could see deep into the still water. The pool was very full, even running over a little into the rushes that grew around it. The water was so clear that Nathan knew it must be pure. He put his face down and drank from it thirstily. It tasted good. Then he raised his head and watched the circles on the surface of the pool widen until the water was quiet again. Even though it was clear, the water was too deep for Nathan to see the bottom of the pool.

The Pool

Instead, he saw his own face looking back at him. It looked happy, and Nathan laughed aloud to make it look still more happy. Then a voice spoke behind him and Nathan turned quickly to look up into the face of Jesus. He was smiling.

"Give me a drink from your pool, Nathan," he was saying. And because there was nothing else to drink from, Nathan put his hands into the cool water and held them up in the shape of a cup that Jesus might lean down and drink from them. Then Jesus knelt and putting his own hands in the pool he passed them gently over Nathan's face and head. "Let your heart be like the pool, my son," he said. "You are happy to see it filled by the rains and overflowing with fresh, clear water. Happy are they whose hearts are pure and overflowing with love. The loving-kindness of God will fill them as showers fill up the springs that feed the pool. And remember this, Nathan, when you look into a heart which is pure and overflowing with love, it will not be your own face that you will see. It will be the face of God."

Before Anna and Simeon unrolled their sleeping mats for the night, Anna leaned down to pull up the covers which had fallen off the two boys. "They are not quiet even in their sleep," she said. "Come here, Simeon, and see how Nathan is smiling. He is having pleasant dreams."

Simeon looked lovingly down on his son. "He is a happy little lad," he said.

Chapter viii

THE HILLSIDE

"Happy the makers of peace"

O N   A   M O R N I N G in the early spring, when the sky was as blue as blossoms on the flax, or thistles which grew on the hills, Nathan ran down to the beach to get some fish for his mother. Fishermen had been out all night and their boats were heavy with a good catch. Nathan waited, with others who had come on the same errand, while the fish were being sorted and made ready to sell.

The Hillside

Many of them would go to the markets in the city. Many more would be taken to places where they could be salted and sent to far-off countries on the backs of camels, or even in ships, to such great cities as Athens and Rome. But some of the fish would go right into the ovens of the plain folk of Capernaum who bought them as they first came, cool and dripping, from the waters of the Sea of Galilee.

As he watched the fishermen, busy at their work, Nathan thought of those other men, Peter and Andrew, James and John, who had left their fishing boats to follow Jesus. His eyes searched the shore and he could see Peter's boat swinging at anchor not far away. Its sails were neatly furled and Nathan thought it looked lonely. Many months had now passed since the boat had been used. Peter and the others had gone away to do a different kind of work. Jesus had sent them to spread the Good News of the Kingdom all through the land. He had made them his messengers and given them power to heal the sick and teach people how to be happy.

It was hard for Nathan to imagine Peter's hands, so rough and strong from pulling in his nets, gentle enough to help the suffering. Nor could he think of that quick, impatient tongue speaking words such as Nathan had heard from the lips of Jesus. Yet Nathan remembered hearing his father tell of how, when Jesus had called Peter, Andrew, James and John from their boats, he had said he would make them "fishers of men." Nathan laughed. Jesus always knew how to make people understand. He meant that he would teach them how to make nets of healing and loving-kindness which would draw people into the Kingdom. That was what they were doing now.

And not only the fishermen had followed Jesus. There were the rest of the twelve men whom Jesus had chosen to do this work. Nathan counted on his fingers: Matthew, the tax-collector, had gone with Thomas; Philip and Nathaniel had gone together; the other James with Thaddeus; and Simon with Judas Iscariot. They had gone two and two so they would all have company on their journey. Nathan looked over toward Peter's house which stood at a little distance from the shore. When Jesus came back to Capernaum that house would be nearly hidden by the crowds that would gather as soon as it was known he was there. Every time he came the crowds grew bigger and bigger. Peter and his family, as well as others who were closest to him, worried because Jesus had no time to rest.

As Nathan was looking at Peter's house, a boy came out and started to run in his direction. Nathan thought it was Juda and ran to meet him. But when he came nearer he could see that the boy was Eber, the son of Matthew. Nathan slowed his steps and waited for Eber to come up. He did not feel as eager to see him as he would have felt if the boy had been Juda. This was because Matthew, Eber's father, had been a tax-collector.

All Jewish children could see the dislike which was shown by the older people for the men who took taxes at the customs office. These taxes had to be paid by all caravans passing through Capernaum from the east or west, and were given to Rome. Sometimes the men who collected them

The Hillside

kept part of the money for themselves and became rich. Matthew had been a rich man with a large house before he left his place at the customs to follow Jesus. Nathan felt that when Matthew became a friend of Jesus it must have been because his hunger for goodness was greater than his greed for money, but many people did not understand. Nathan had heard his father say that the leaders in the synagogue did not like it that Jesus had made a friend of Matthew. They grumbled about his choice of friends anyway. But Simeon had said that Jesus saw only the heart of a man, no matter whether he were priest or sinner in the eyes of others. It was clear to Nathan that Matthew's heart had changed, to make him ready to leave everything else for the work of the Kingdom.

Nathan was remembering all this as he waited for Eber, and he felt so ashamed that he looked down and began to kick at the sand with his foot. But, somehow, he didn't like to play with Eber as much as he did with Juda. It was not a nice feeling, Nathan thought uncomfortably, and it really had nothing to do with Eber himself. It was mostly because he had heard the other children call Eber names and tease him. Nathan would not do that, of course. But, he had to be honest with himself, it was so easy to follow what the other children did in a crowd that he couldn't feel quite sure that he would not be guilty of doing the same thing.

Eber did not see Nathan until he was quite close. Then he stopped and greeted him. "Hello, Nathan," he said. "Do you want to know where I'm going?"

He sounded as though he were going somewhere very

special, so Nathan asked with interest, "Where are you going, Eber?"

"I am going a long way," answered Eber, "to spend the night, or perhaps two nights, with my cousin who is a shepherd. His sheep are pastured across the lake, beyond the Jordan near Bethsaida Julius."

Nathan knew this was five miles away and he was surprised that Eber was walking so far alone, but Eber soon explained this. "I am going in a boat most of the way," he said. "Jesse, the fisherman, has promised to take me. See," said Eber, opening his basket, "I have fresh bread which my mother gave me and I will get some fish from Jesse. My cousin will cook them and we shall have enough food for two days at least. Would you like to go with me, Nathan?" Eber asked.

"I can't," said Nathan, "because I have to take some fish home, and then I have to go to school. But I hope you will have a good time, Eber."

Eber's face clouded a little. Some of the children in the synagogue school had made him unhappy so his father had someone teach him at home. Nathan was sorry he had spoken about school and hurried to ask Eber what he had been doing at Simon Peter's house.

Eber came a little closer and spoke in a low voice so that no one but Nathan could hear. "I took a message from my father," he said. "He came home last night. Jesus is back at Peter's house, but you must not tell anyone because Sara says he needs rest from the crowds that have followed him everywhere."

The Hillside

Nathan's heart felt a thrill of joy. "Did you see Jesus, Eber?" he asked eagerly.

"Yes," Eber answered, and his face lighted up again. "Look," he drew a little wooden boat from his belt, "he made this for me. He carved it out of a block of wood while I was there."

Nathan had seen Jesus make toys for children many times. He remembered how swift and sure his hands were, and how smooth and perfect were the things he carved from wood. Sara said it was because Jesus had been a carpenter, but Nathan thought that anything his hands touched seemed to grow into the same perfection as the little toys he gave to the children. Nathan had a bird and Juda a camel which Jesus had made for them. Nathan took the boat which Eber held out to him. For an instant he felt sorry that he had not seen Jesus first. Perhaps then the boat would have been carved for him instead of Eber. But he knew this was not a very kind thought, and Eber was waiting for him to say what a nice toy Jesus had made for him, so Nathan's face cleared and he smiled as he handled the little boat. Just passing his fingers over the smooth sides, and putting them into the places which had been carved out by Jesus's fingers a short time before, gave him pleasure. It made him feel more friendly with Eber, too. "It's a fine boat," he said. "If you put a stick for a mast and a piece of cloth for a sail it would go fast."

"Maybe you would sail it with me some day, Nathan," said Eber, putting the boat away again in the folds of his tunic. "We could go to one of the coves where the wind would not blow it too far."

"Yes," said Nathan, "we'll go when you come back from visiting your cousin."

As Eber ran off Nathan felt happy in this new friendliness with him. Somehow, when Jesus was near, people became friends more easily. Nathan longed to run over to Peter's house and forget his errand on the beach, but he knew if he did he would feel ashamed of himself the moment Jesus looked at him. It would not be kind to leave his mother waiting for the fish. Then there was school. For almost the first time Nathan did not want to go to school. Then he remembered that Juda would be there and would tell him more about Jesus.

It did not take Nathan long to get his fish, for the fishermen were now ready to sell them. As he hurried home he wondered whether he should tell his mother what Eber had told him. Surely Eber had not meant him to keep this secret from his mother and father. Besides, they would never spread the news and make it hard for Jesus to rest. They were among those friends who tried so hard to spare him. But when Nathan reached home, and repeated what he had heard from Eber, he found that his mother already knew.

"Yes, little son," said Anna, "Sara has told me about the Master's return. He is tired from the crowds that pressed him for healing and teaching while he was away. They will gather again as soon as it is known that he is in Capernaum, so you must help us keep the secret until he is ready."

"Are Simon Peter and Andrew back, too, Mother?" asked

The Hillside

Nathan, feeling a bit disappointed that he had not been the first to bring the news. "Eber said his father came home last night."

"Yes," said Anna, "Andrew and Peter also came back last night. I think all the friends who have been away are in their homes again. They will be meeting to tell Jesus about their travels, so you must not go to Peter's house and put yourself in their way, Nathan."

"I wouldn't do that, you know I wouldn't, Mother!" cried Nathan. So Anna drew him to her and explained that she had not meant to hurt him, but only to warn him against doing anything to spoil the quiet talks which Jesus and his friends might wish to have together.

At the synagogue school that morning the rabbi had to rap several times to bring Nathan's wandering thoughts back to his lessons. Juda, too, was scolded once or twice for his inattention. Once they both were caught making signs at each other and had to listen with shamed faces to some very sharp words from the rabbi. But when the Scroll of Isaiah was taken from the chest where the Sacred Scrolls were kept, and the rabbi began to read the words which the boys would repeat after him, Nathan joined very heartily with the others, for they were words he loved.

> "The people that walked in darkness
> Have seen a great light:"

The words seemed to ring deep down in his heart like bells. He did not know why, but it was always that way with these words. To see a great light after walking in darkness! That must be wonderful. Suppose a blind man suddenly should be able to see! Nathan's lips went on repeating after the rabbi while his thoughts raced ahead because he knew the words so well:

> "For unto us a child is born
> Unto us a son is given,"

The light would come because of a child being born, thought Nathan. Children *were* important, then. Jesus had said they had something to do with the Kingdom.

> "And the government shall be upon his shoulder. . . ."

Perhaps that meant the government of the kingdom. Nathan knew what the wise man who had written the Scroll of Isaiah was talking about, because his mother and father had explained it to him. All good Jews were looking for the time when their people would be free from the rule of foreign governors and could set up a kingdom of their own with a king once more upon the throne of David. But this could not be until the coming of the great leader whom they called Messiah. The prophet, Isaiah, was telling about the coming of this leader, but Nathan did not think the words sounded like the kind of leader the Jews expected. Nathan repeated slowly with the other boys:

> "And his name shall be called Wonderful, Counsellor. . . .
> The Prince of Peace. . . ."

The Hillside

Prince of Peace — Nathan loved the sound of that name. A child who should grow up to become the ruler of the new Kingdom and should be called the Prince of Peace. He would not be a warrior-king. He would be a Prince of Peace.

If the rabbi had been watching Nathan just then, he would have seen that his lips had stopped moving and his mouth was open as though he had suddenly thought of something, as indeed he had. Nathan was remembering how Jesus had said: "Happy are the makers of peace." He was remembering the times he had seen Jesus come into a room or join a group of people with the quiet greeting, "Peace be with you." He was seeing again how faces changed from sad, suffering faces to faces of peace and joy as Jesus talked about the Kingdom. Yes, thought Nathan, with a feeling of wonder, *that* was the Kingdom the writer of the Scroll of Isaiah meant, and Jesus was the Prince of Peace.

As Nathan and Juda ran home together, Juda told Nathan that his father and Andrew had come home, and that all the men who had been preaching the good news of the kingdom were back. "I heard them talking with Jesus," said Juda, "and they told of wonderful things, Nathan. Come home with me and maybe, if we creep in very quietly, we may listen to their stories."

But Nathan had caught sight of a now familiar and pitiful little company of people, moving in the direction of Peter's house. One man was carried on a blanket by four others. Another limped on crutches, and some were blind and felt their way with a cane or by holding the arm of a friend.

"Look," he cried, pointing out this group to Juda, "some-one has told them Jesus is here."

The boys stopped and looked around the market place which they had been crossing. Yes, out of every street men, women, and children were beginning to pour. They were not all townspeople, but looked to Nathan as though they had come from many towns around the lake. Some, from the farther away cities, had probably been traveling all night. Storekeepers came to the front of their shops to watch, and talked among themselves.

"Come," said Juda, pulling at Nathan's sleeve, "let's get there ahead of them." But it was no use. Even when they tried to slip around through back streets they found the crowd was ahead of them. So they had to dodge in and out, and duck under elbows, until they finally reached the lake. Here the crowd was not in front of Peter's house as they had expected. People were standing along the shore, and their eyes were following a boat which was rapidly gather-ing headway as the wind filled its sail. Nathan wondered for a moment what it was that made all eyes follow it so eagerly. Then he saw that Peter's boat was missing. "Juda," he cried, "it is your father's boat. Jesus and all of them have gone."

"Let us ask my mother," said Juda, running off toward home. But Nathan did not follow him. He had caught sight of Joseph who worked on his father's farm. Joseph was with a group of young men. They were talking excitedly, so Nathan got close enough to hear what they were saying. These young men, too, were gazing after the boat which was getting smaller and smaller as the wind bore it farther from the shore.

"He may be going away for good," said Joseph, "and just when we had planned to make him our king."

"He is going to another land where Herod will have no power to put him to death as he did John the Baptizer," said another.

"But if we make him our king," said a third, "we shall fight our enemies and drive them out. We shall build again the kingdom of Israel. Jesus of Nazareth is a great leader. See how the people follow him."

"We must go after him," said Joseph, "and bring him back. Now is the time. We should crown him in Jerusalem at the Feast of Passover."

"Let us get a boat and go after them," cried two or three of the men.

By this time other people were listening, for their voices had become very loud. The word began to pass along through the crowd: "He has gone away — Jesus has gone away." Nathan could see tears rolling down the cheeks of some of the women. One, who stood near him, held a little boy who could not walk, and Nathan thought of what Jesus had done for Enoch. "Let us bring him back," he shouted, repeating the words he had heard Joseph speak. Soon other voices took up the cry, and the crowd began to surge along the shore toward the northern end of the lake.

Joseph and his friends ran to the water's edge where one of them had a boat anchored in the shallows. They waded in and scrambled over the side. Nathan did not stop to think about whether they would let him go or not, he felt only that he must go with the others and bring Jesus back. So he ran after the men and pulled himself into the boat with them. He had been out with fishermen many times and knew how to tuck himself into a small space where he would be out of the way, so no one noticed him until the sail had been run up and the boat was well out from shore. Then it was too late to send him back, and Joseph and his friends were so full of their own plans that Nathan got only the mildest of scoldings and was soon forgotten entirely.

As they sailed over the blue water, Nathan could see people running along the north shore of the lake. Behind him they were still pouring out of the streets of the city. It made him think of a great flock of sheep who had lost their shepherd. Those people were not looking for a warrior-king who would lead them into battle, they wanted someone who would be like a good shepherd and lead them into ways of peace.

Nathan wrinkled his forehead as he wondered what peace really meant. Did it mean doing nothing? Would all those people, who worked on the sea or in the fields, want to stop and do nothing? Would that be peace? Nathan didn't think so. No, peace was a feeling, but it was not a lazy feeling. Jesus did not put people to sleep, he made them feel more alive! He made them happy and friendly.

Nathan had been thinking so hard that he was surprised when he felt the bottom of the boat scraping on the sand while tall reeds brushed against his face. Joseph and another of the young men jumped out in the shallow water and pulled the boat farther up on the shore. "Look," cried Joseph, "there is Simon Peter's boat. They must have gone this way. We shall find them somewhere in the hills."

Nathan scrambled out, his heart beating fast, and followed the men as they struck out across the countryside. The grass was thick and green. It felt soft and cool to his feet. After they had gone some distance, Nathan was not surprised to see a flock of sheep grazing on the side of a hill. It was the sort of pasture a good shepherd would choose. Joseph called to the shepherd to ask if he had seen anyone pass that way, and a boy came running at the sound of his voice. Nathan saw that it was Eber, and he remembered that Eber had said he was going to stay with his cousin who was a shepherd.

"No," said the shepherd, "I have seen no one, but the people you are looking for might have gone around the other side of the hill where they would be out of sight."

Eber looked surprised to see Nathan and stood staring after him as he ran off with the men. Nathan wanted to tell him who it was they were looking for, but he didn't know whether Joseph would like it.

A few moments later, as they were climbing the slope of another hill, Joseph stopped suddenly and pointed toward the summit. There they were, Jesus and his disciples; but they were still too far away to have noticed the young men who were looking for them. Nathan could see that they were talking together as on that first day he had seen Jesus. He hoped Joseph and the others would not disturb them. Joseph watched for a moment in silence and then turned to his friends. "Let us wait here," he said, and Nathan thought his face looked ashamed, "They will not go away without our seeing them, so we will leave them in peace for a while."

Nathan could not help saying: "The other people will get here soon, Joseph, all those people who ran around the lake. Couldn't we stop them?"

"Stop them!" Joseph answered scornfully, "you might as well try to stop a sand storm on the desert. Lie down on the grass, Nathan, and be quiet. Remember we did not ask you to come with us. It will not be good for me with your father if he thinks I let you come without first telling your mother."

Nathan obeyed Joseph. His legs were tired and it felt good to drop down on the soft grass. He knew he had not stopped to think when he had followed the men into the boat at Capernaum, but he felt he could no more have kept from doing it than he could have helped following the crowd that day to the hills behind Capernaum. Nathan rolled over and raised himself on his elbows so he could look up the hill. He could see the heads of Jesus and his disciples against the blue of the sky. Joseph had said to leave them in peace. Yet Joseph didn't know that Jesus was the Prince of Peace. He wanted to make him a warrior-king. The wind blew through the grass and made it wave back and forth. The greenness seemed to flow around them like water, and its coolness made Nathan feel as though he had been washed clean of every feeling but happiness. The men were quiet, too, sitting with their eyes watching the group

The Hillside

on the hill. Some of them chewed the long pieces of grass.

All at once Joseph jumped up and pointed to where they could see the Jordan River flowing down to the Sea of Galilee. Crossing it on stones, or just splashing through from one bank to the other, were the firstcomers of those whom Nathan had seen from the boat running around the lake shore. "There they come," cried Joseph. "You can't keep the crowds away from Jesus. We will make him a great king."

Nathan sat up to see better, then he looked back again at the group on the hill. Had Jesus seen these people coming? Would he be angry with them for following? Nathan could see that all heads had turned toward the river and that Jesus and his friends were watching the approach of the crowd.

"Let us go closer," said Joseph starting up the hill. His friends followed him and Nathan ran along, trying to keep up with their long strides. As they went higher up the hill, they could see the whole plain below, over which the crowd was hurrying. The people had seen Jesus on the hill and were running and scrambling across the fields after fording the river. As they swarmed up the slope, Nathan was close enough to see that Jesus was watching them with a sad face. Even the disciples did not look angry at being interrupted, although their quiet day was spoiled. They, too, looked with pity on the people who needed Jesus so badly that they had come all this distance to find him.

Jesus waited until most of the people had come close enough to hear him. Then he asked them to sit on the grass, while he seated himself a little higher up where they could see and hear him. The disciples sat near by, and Nathan crept as close as he dared. After a moment another boy lay down beside him, and Nathan saw that it was Eber. His cousin, the shepherd, had joined Joseph and his friends.

Then Jesus began to speak and all the noise died away. There was only the sound of his voice and the soft murmur of the wind in the grass. Sometimes a cripple or a sick person was carried through the crowd and put before Jesus. Nathan saw how the pain left their faces as Jesus placed his hands upon them. He saw other faces change, too, as though the people had been made well inside; as though their thoughts and hearts had been healed, thought Nathan. The afternoon passed and it was getting dark, but still the great company showed no sign of going away. Now the disciples began to speak to each other quietly. Nathan saw that they looked worried. Then they spoke to Jesus and pointed to the shadows.

"I think," whispered Eber to Nathan, "that they want people to go home to their supper. See, Nathan, I have enough in my pouch for you if you are hungry. Here are five loaves and two fishes. I shall still have enough left for my lunch tomorrow."

Nathan did feel hungry and he thought it was very friendly of Eber to offer to share his food with him. Home seemed a long way off, and he hadn't noticed Joseph or his friends carrying anything to eat. So Nathan thanked Eber and felt happy in discovering what a nice boy Eber really was. But Andrew had been looking around at those who

The Hillside

were near him and his eyes were now upon Eber. He spoke to Jesus and then beckoned to Eber who jumped up and went to him. Nathan saw Jesus smile at Eber and hold out his hands. Andrew took the pouch containing Eber's lunch and gave it to Jesus. Nathan gasped. To share with Jesus would be wonderful! Oh, if only he, too, had brought something with him!

However, Jesus was not eating the lunch. He had lifted his head so that his eyes were looking up at the sky. He was talking to God. He was asking God to bless Eber's food. Then Nathan saw Jesus break the loaves and fishes into pieces and give some to Andrew and Peter and all the disciples to pass to the crowd. In and out they went among the people, giving each one something to eat. Nathan felt as though his eyes would pop out of his head as he watched Eber's lunch feeding so many.

Eber came running back and dropped down beside Nathan. "I gave my lunch to Jesus, Nathan," he cried breathlessly, "and do you see how he is making it enough for everyone to have a share? It was such a small lunch, too."

"What are you saying, boy?" asked Joseph who had moved over and grasped Eber's shoulder. "There are fully five thousand people here, and you think your lunch can feed them?" But even while he was asking the question, Peter came and offered them their share, and all their voices were stilled with the wonder of it.

Then Joseph jumped to his feet and called to his followers: "This is a new Moses who feeds his people in a desert place. This is the expected leader. He has the power of

God. We will make him our king now!" Joseph's voice reached many people and his words were carried from mouth to mouth through the multitude. They began to press closer to Jesus, shouting for him to be their king. Nathan and Eber felt a little frightened and stood close together. Nathan could see Jesus talking with his friends. In a few moments the disciples started down the hill toward the lake, leaving Jesus alone with the crowd.

"Go in peace," Jesus said, and as he spoke all the tumult died. "I will come again to you, but I must be alone now." Then he went off toward the hills beyond, and people began to turn toward their homes.

But Joseph would not go. He and his friends decided to wait until morning and see Jesus again before he returned to Capernaum. "If we see him alone," said Joseph, "we can make him listen to us."

"He will never be your king," cried Nathan, "because he is the Prince of Peace." A big sob choked him as he saw he could not make them understand.

Joseph was looking at him with a frown. "What do you know, little one?" he asked not unkindly. "It would be better if you did not listen so much to old people and women who are content to live under the rule of Roman governors."

The other men began to grumble. "Send the boy home, Joseph," said one. "We don't want him here all night."

Nathan swallowed hard. For the first time that afternoon he thought about his home. He wanted to go home, but who would take him? It was a long way. Then he felt

The Hillside

Eber's hand slip into his. "Come with me, Nathan," he said. "My cousin will look out for you."

"He should go home," said Joseph, uneasily. "If you run along with some of the people who are going to Capernaum you will be all right, Nathan."

But someone else had come up while Joseph was speaking, and Nathan heard a familiar voice saying: "I will take care of my son, Joseph." It was Simeon, and the grip of his father's hand on his shoulder made Nathan feel very safe.

Eber said goodbye and ran back to help the shepherd call his sheep, while Nathan and his father started for home. It was almost dark when they got to the river. Simeon lifted Nathan as though he had been Enoch and forded the river with him in his arms. There were others crossing at the same time, and someone started to sing the lovely song of David: "The Lord is my shepherd." Soon all were singing. Nathan wondered if their voices reached that place where Jesus had gone alone. He hoped so, because then Jesus would know that everyone was happy and friendly.

His father's arms felt good to Nathan and he clasped his own more tightly around his father's neck. He remembered how Jesus had said God was the Father of everybody. He had taught his friends to pray: "Our Father which art in heaven." Jesus knew how people would feel if they could talk to God as a Father. They would not be afraid. They would have only love in their hearts. Nathan knew that after a while he would talk with his father about coming so far from home, and staying away so long. He would have to explain, but he would not be afraid. His father would understand. He would know that Nathan was sorry for his thoughtlessness. Even if he spoke sternly, there would still be love between them.

The wind was making a moaning sound. It blew the loose tunics and cloaks worn by the people, tightly about their legs and shoulders. It ruffled the water of the river so that it splashed against them. Down on the lake the water would be getting very rough, thought Nathan, and he was glad he was not going back by boat. He looked up and saw how the clouds were racing across the sky, making a long veil to hide the brightness of the new moon.

Nathan thought of Peter, James and John, and the other disciples who were by this time in their boat on the way to Capernaum. He thought of Jesus alone under the trees. He thought of Joseph and the other young men waiting until morning for him to come back so they could make him a king of Israel, not knowing that he was the Prince of Peace.

Nathan thought of Eber who would wrap himself in his cloak and sleep close to the shepherd tonight. Eber had been his friend. Eber had been the friend of everyone when he shared his lunch. Jesus had been able to feed five thousand people because one boy was willing to share his lunch. People can't help being friends, thought Nathan, when they share bread with each other. And when they are friends, there is peace.

"Father," said Nathan, when they had reached the shore and Simeon let him slip out of his arms to the ground, "Joseph and some of the crowd want to make Jesus a king, and put him upon the throne of David in Jerusalem."

The Hillside

"I know, my son," answered Simeon quietly.

"But he doesn't want to be that kind of king, Father. I know he doesn't. He is the Prince of Peace."

"I think you have spoken truly, little Nathan," said Simeon. "It is not that kind of kingdom Jesus and his friends are working for. It is a kingdom where all people shall live in love and peace. God, our Father, will be the only ruler."

"And all who make peace will belong to the Kingdom, Father, because Jesus said: 'Happy are the makers of peace for they shall be called God's children.' "

"Yes," said Simeon, drawing Nathan close so he could shield him from the cold wind with his cloak, "yes, always remember that, my son."

Nathan thought again: the makers of peace are those who share what they have with others, the kind, friendly people. He thought again of Eber who would share with him the little boat which Jesus had made, his lunch, or his bed on the slope of a hill. Eber was his friend and Nathan was happy.

Chapter ix

STANDING UP FOR
A FRIEND

"Happy those who are persecuted for their goodness"

I T WAS a tired boy who returned to Capernaum that
night. The walk home had been long, and the wind
had blown up one of the sudden storms which sometimes
lifted the quiet waters of the lake into great waves with
foaming crests that beat upon the shore. Nathan and his
father were wet and cold when they reached home, but
Anna was waiting to make them comfortable. She no sooner
wiped the rain from Nathan's face and hair, and slipped a

dry tunic over his head, than he rolled over on the mat beside little Enoch and was fast asleep. Simeon and Anna talked softly far into the night but Nathan did not stir.

It was Juda who told Nathan the story of how Peter's boat had been nearly wrecked in the storm that night. Juda told him how his father and the other disciples had labored with the oars to keep their boat from being overturned by the fury of the wind and waves. When they were worn out with the struggle, the voice of Jesus had come to them out of the darkness telling them to have courage. He had followed them along the beach, and, when the boat had been blown close to the shore, he had called to them. At first, Juda said, they were frightened because they could not see who it was that had called, but Jesus had walked out and climbed into the boat, and right away they found themselves in quieter water with the wind dropping as quickly as it had risen. They had been able to row again, Juda went on, but, instead of stopping at Capernaum, had gone on toward Magdala. On the little quiet beach where they landed, two or three fishermen had seen Jesus and had hurried off to tell others he was there. Soon the crowd was gathering again.

Now, Nathan knew, Jesus was back in Capernaum teaching in the synagogue. He was talking with the leaders of the synagogue and answering their questions. Some wise men, called scribes, had come to Capernaum from Jerusalem to find out what he was saying. Nathan heard his father talking with Jairus about it. They thought these men had been sent by Herod to spy on Jesus. Herod wanted them to find some fault which would give him an excuse to punish Jesus and stop his teaching.

Jairus thought Jesus ought to go where he would not be in danger from Herod, some place where Herod could not deal with him as he had with John, the Baptizer. Nathan grew cold when he heard Jairus say this, and, for the first time, he wanted to have Jesus go away. He wanted to beg his father and Jairus to ask Jesus to go where he would be safe, but Nathan knew better than to interrupt when older people were talking. So, although his fear nearly choked him, he ran off to the market place where he was always sure of finding other children at play. He must get rid of this ache in his heart. Why should anyone want to harm Jesus who brought so much happiness?

Nathan found the market place full of all kinds of people. That was what made it so exciting. There were plenty of traders today and the shops of the merchants were busy. Caravans going east and west jostled each other at the customs office where they paid their taxes. Nathan stopped to put his hand on the rough side of a little donkey, but a camel moved in and he jumped out of the way.

There were peddlers, too, who always came north in the spring, bringing in their baskets pretty things to sell which would catch the eye of the women and girls. Nathan saw Renah and her friend, Esther, looking at a scarf which one of these men was holding up. He thought if he had some money he would like to buy one for each of the girls. A bright scarf would look pretty on their dark hair. He poked his head between them to look into the basket. No, he would

buy a bracelet for one, and a jar of that scented oil for the other.

"Oh, Nathan," cried Renah when she saw who was crowding her, "we have been looking for you everywhere. Enoch wants to play with you. Do you see him? He was here a minute ago."

Nathan felt that Enoch might be in the way if he wanted to get in a game with some of the older boys, and he said so to Renah. "Why don't you keep him with you?" he asked.

"Because he would rather play with you," Renah told him. "It isn't much fun for him to stay with us. Look, there he is."

Enoch came running across the street. He had a fig in his hand which someone had given him, and his face was all smiles when he saw Nathan. It suddenly popped into Nathan's mind how much he meant to his little brother. The thought made him feel kinder toward Enoch, and all at once he remembered what Jesus had said that day when he was telling him about Enoch's fall. Jesus had said that God entrusted the care of his small, helpless children to those who were able to take care of them. Perhaps that was what God expected of big brothers. He trusted them to look out for little brothers and sisters and be kind to them.

"All right," said Nathan slowly, for it was hard to give up his own plans. "He can come with me." Esther smiled at him and it gave Nathan a warm feeling around his heart. He was glad he had not quarreled with Renah about Enoch and made everyone unhappy, most of all himself. He took half of the fig which Enoch wanted to share with him, and they

Standing Up For a Friend

ran off together leaving the girls to turn back to the peddler's basket. Nathan thought he would like to buy two presents for Esther, but, as little boys did not often have a coin to spend, he laughed to think how silly he was. Enoch laughed, too, just because Nathan was laughing. So they went on in high good humor.

They had not gone far before Nathan began to notice people standing in groups of three or four, talking earnestly. He and Enoch all the time seemed to be going around these groups. Nathan looked up into the faces of some of these men. They were mostly men who might have been coming from the synagogue, he thought. They looked gloomy and disappointed. Then he saw Joseph and some of the young men who had wanted to make Jesus their warrior-king that day on the hillside. Nathan wondered if they had spent the night there. He thought they must have been very much disappointed when morning came and Jesus was not there because he had already joined his disciples in the boat and gone to the other side of the lake. Nathan pulled Enoch's hand to make him wait a moment so that he might hear what Joseph was saying. Joseph's face was dark with anger, but Nathan thought he looked tired and puzzled, too.

"He is not the man I thought he was," said Joseph. "When he fed the multitude over on the hillside he seemed like another Moses who had power from God and could feed his people with bread from heaven. I looked for him to do even greater things. But now he says the true bread from heaven is not like the manna which our fathers ate in the desert. The true bread, which comes from God and gives life to the world, is found in him and what he teaches."

"How can people be fed on words?" asked one of the others.

Well, thought Nathan, he had seen people look as though they were being fed by Jesus's words. He had watched their faces change while he was speaking. It was as though they were being filled with food that brought them life and joy. Nathan could not tell why it was, but he had felt the same way himself. It was a kind of happiness that ran all through you, like the little streams that watered the roots of the vines and made sap run through the dry branches until, suddenly, they were different. The vines were no longer dead-looking but were covered with blossoms or fruit.

Joseph was saying: "If he will not be our king, we'll have to look for another. Let us get back to our work."

Nathan thought his father would be very glad to see Joseph out on the farm, for he was needed there. But Enoch was tugging at his hand and begging him to come and play, so Nathan left the young men who were so anxious for Jesus to be a leader of the Jewish nation, and looked around for some friends of their own ages.

In one of the narrow streets which opened on the market place, he saw some boys and girls who seemed to be having a good time dancing to tunes which they played on little reed pipes. Nathan knew they were pretending to have a wedding. This was a game all children liked, because weddings were a time for music and dancing, and all kinds of merrymaking. Some of the boys were sitting in a line as they had seen their fathers do at wedding feasts. They had little cups of water in front of them, and figs to eat. Some of the girls had formed a circle as their mothers and other women did, and all the rest of the children danced and made their piping music around them.

It was great fun, and Nathan and Enoch were not long in joining them. Most of the boys were Nathan's schoolmates so they knew Nathan and were glad to let him take part in their game. They did not mind having Enoch, either, for he could dance around with the dancers. The more dancing and noise there was, the more fun it would be. At real weddings, guests always brought food for the feast, so Nathan was glad his mother had given him some small cakes to slip into his tunic when she had taken her baking from the oven that day. He brought them out now and put them with the figs and water. Everyone shouted with joy at this addition to their feast.

So the game went on happily for a while. Then some began to tire of it and look around for something else to do. "Look," cried Jared, one of the older boys, "there is Eber the son of Matthew, who got rich from collecting taxes. What is he carrying in his arms?"

Nathan stopped what he was doing and looked to where Jared was pointing. Eber had come up quietly and had been watching them play. He had a baby lamb which he was holding in the folds of his tunic. Nathan thought his cousin, the shepherd, must have given it to him.

"It's a lamb," cried another boy. "Let's kill it and use it for a sacrifice."

Nathan saw Eber clasp the lamb more tightly to him

while a look of fear came over his face. But he did not run.

"No, no," Nathan heard a girl's voice saying, "don't hurt the lamb!"

"All right," said Jared laughing, "let's play sheep and wolves. Eber shall be the sheep and we'll be the wolves that chase him. Start running, old sheep."

Several of the children howled like wolves, and some leaned down to pick up small stones with which to make the chase more exciting. Nathan knew that this would not be a nice game. It was an excuse to tease Eber and, perhaps, hurt him. And Eber was his friend. Eber had shared all he had with him on the hillside. Nathan knew he not only could not join in this game, he must stand beside Eber and show the others that he was Eber's friend. He did not wait any longer but ran over to where Eber already was having his tunic jerked by two or three hungry "wolves." "I will be a sheep, too," cried Nathan.

Eber had turned and was on the point of getting away as swiftly as possible, but he stopped when he saw Nathan and a glad light came into his face. The rest of the children looked at Nathan in surprise.

"Get out of the way, Nathan," shouted Jared, "we want only one sheep."

"No," said Nathan. And then he saw that Enoch had pushed his way close to him and was holding his hand. He had not thought about little Enoch's getting hurt. He had thought that he and Eber could run and hide among the booths in the market place, but Enoch's legs were too short. He would hold them back.

Standing Up For a Friend

"Three sheep!" called another boy. "Come on, let's chase them." And someone threw a stone.

Nathan stepped in front of Enoch and the stone hit him on his forehead. It stung badly and he could feel a warm trickle of blood running into his eye. He put up his hand to wipe it away. Eber cried out and Nathan felt him press close against him. Then, suddenly, there was the sound of running feet. The "wolves" were not chasing them, they were running away. Nathan felt a cool hand on his head. He opened one eye and put back his head to look up. Jesus was smiling down at him. "What was the trouble, son?" he asked. And Nathan knew that this time he need not be ashamed.

But it was Eber who told Jesus, and Peter and John who were with him, what had happened. It was Peter who had sent the children flying, while John had comforted Enoch and picked up the little bleating lamb, which Eber had dropped in his fear for Nathan. While Eber was telling what had happened, Jesus asked John to get some water so he could wash the blood from Nathan's face. His fingers seemed to soothe and heal the cut forehead so that all the sting and ache were soon gone. Perhaps, thought Nathan, the happiness in his heart was so great he could not feel anything else.

When Eber had finished, Jesus took Nathan's face between his hands and looked into his eyes as he said: "You were hurt for being true to a friend, Nathan, yet you are not unhappy?"

Nathan could not find the right words to say all he

135

felt, but he knew Jesus could read his answer in his eyes.

Jesus went on talking. "It is like that with all who suffer for their goodness, my child," he said. "It can only bring them joy." After a moment he added, as though speaking to himself: "Happy those who are persecuted for their goodness; the Kingdom of Heaven is theirs."

Nathan could not know then that a few years later a man, named Stephen, would be stoned to death for being true to his friend, Jesus of Nazareth, and that it would be said of him that his face was so happy it was like the face of an angel. But Nathan wondered what Jesus was seeing when he let his hands drop at his sides and raised his eyes to the western sky. He looked as though he were gazing at a picture no one else could see. The sounds in the market place faded away and it seemed very quiet. Nathan thought of a line from the Book of Praise: "Be still, and know that I am God."

Then Peter broke the silence. "Master," he said, "shall we not send the children home now? It is growing late."

"Yes, you must go to your homes, little ones," said Jesus, turning his face back to them and resting his hand once more on Nathan's head. "And, Nathan, you have pleased me very much. It is not always easy to be true when you know it will cost you pain, but it shows that friendship and goodness mean more than anything else."

Nathan felt he could hardly bear such praise from Jesus because there were so many times when he was not like that. "Master," he said, slowly, "I am not always a good boy. I make trouble for my mother and father by running away sometimes. And I do not always listen to the rabbi in the synagogue school because my eyes are looking out of the window. Besides" — Nathan felt he must tell Jesus this — "it was Eber who made me his friend by being kind to me first."

"You are both children of the Kingdom," said Jesus, putting out his other hand to draw Eber closer. Then he added: "The ways of a child, Nathan, are often unthinking ways, because he has not yet learned to think before he acts. So he must be guided by his parents or those who have his care at heart, or he causes trouble. But when a time comes, as it came to you today, that you do the right thing because you could not do anything else, it is the heart which speaks. And the language of the heart is love. Let the heart speak again tomorrow, Nathan, when you meet the playmates who threw the stone just now. Peter," he said, turning to Peter with a twinkle in his eye, "you should not have driven the boys off so quickly. We might have made friends of them for Eber instead of enemies. Children often forget to be kind when they are playing, and sometimes they are cruel."

Peter laughed his big, hearty laugh as he said: "It was not I but their own wrongdoing that frightened them off, Master. They needed only a word to send them flying."

"They will be sorry tomorrow," said Jesus. Then he turned to Eber. "Your father is a good man, Eber. Never let anyone make you ashamed of him. Those who are unkind to you because he once held a despised office will some day honor you for his work in my Kingdom."

Nathan was glad Jesus had said this about Matthew, Eber's father, for he had often thought what a dreadful thing it would be for a boy to feel ashamed of his father, even though he knew people were wrong about him.

Peter again began to urge Jesus to send the children home, so John gave Eber his lamb and Enoch reached for Nathan's hand. But before they ran off, Nathan stopped and turned back a moment. He took Jesus's hand and pressed it against his cheek. "Thank you, Jesus of Nazareth," he said.

As Nathan and Enoch went home through the market place, the afternoon sun was going down behind the hills and most of the city was in shadow. But a line of gold ran along the hilltops, and every bit of orange and pink in the world, Nathan thought, flamed in the western sky. Most of the people they had seen earlier in the market place were gone now and it was quieter. Travelers were on their way or had found lodgings for the night, and merchants were putting away their wares for another day. One or two stopped and smiled as the children passed, and wondered what had given them that happy light in their eyes.

Anna had supper waiting on the roof-top, for it was now warm enough to live most of the time out-of-doors. Simeon was there, too, and they had met Renah in the courtyard just setting out to find them. Enoch climbed the steps to the roof as fast as he could and ran to his mother with such eagerness to tell her everything at once that no one could understand what he was talking about. Nathan did not say anything. He felt that what had happened that afternoon was so wonderful that he wanted to keep the memory of it undisturbed within his own heart just a little longer. Anna, after a quick look at his face, put her hand gently over

Enoch's lips. "Wait, wait, little one," she said laughing at him, "we will first have our supper and then you and Nathan shall tell us your story."

So Renah poured the water for the cleansing of their hands, and Simeon gave thanks to God for the food they were about to eat. As they ate the evening meal, the color in the western sky faded to soft lilac and gray, and the shadows deepened. Nathan, curled up on the rug beside his father, could see an almost full moon rising in the east. He remembered that this was a very special moon, for it marked the time of the Passover feast. All who were able went to Jerusalem, a journey of more than eighty miles, to celebrate this greatest feast of the year in the Temple. Jewish pilgrims from all the known world would gather there. Probably some of the people Nathan had seen that afternoon in the market place had been on their way.

Ever since the first thin crescent of this Passover moon had appeared, preparations had been going on in many homes so that Pilgrims might start their three-day journey in time to be in Jerusalem before the full of the moon.

When he should be thirteen, or perhaps even twelve, years of age, Nathan thought, he would go to Jerusalem with his father for the Feast of the Passover. It would be wonderful to go to that city, so rich in history, which David, the shepherd king, had won for his people. And to stand within the courts of the great, gold-domed temple, and hear the trumpets, and take part in all the ceremonies of the feast—that would mean he had grown up, that he had become a "Son of the Law" like other boys of his race at that age.

Standing Up For a Friend

"Father," said Nathan, "the Passover moon will be full soon. I wish I could go to Jerusalem for the feast. Shall I have to wait two years?"

Simeon looked at him kindly. "Perhaps next year I shall take you, Nathan," he answered. "You were eleven a few days ago and another year will make you twelve years old. You are a thoughtful boy for your age. But — we shall see."

"Ah, Simeon," said Anna, "do not make him a man too soon."

"Tell me the story of Passover," begged Enoch.

"Not tonight," said his mother, smoothing his curls, "you are much too sleepy. We shall have the story when we eat the Passover supper together here in our own home."

"I know it anyway," chuckled Enoch. "It's about Moses leading our people away from Egypt where they were slaves."

"But there's more to it than that, isn't there, Father?" asked Nathan, thinking of the wealth of stories his father could tell at these times. He was feeling that it would not be too hard to wait one or even two years to go to Jerusalem because they always had such a happy celebration at home.

Anna was asking Simeon if he thought Jesus would go to Jerusalem this year. Nathan thought there was fear in her voice.

"I do not know," answered Simeon. "Many think it would be better if he did not go. But if he stays away it will not be because he is afraid of what Herod may do." How glad Nathan was to hear his father say that, though he had known in his heart it was true. Simeon went on:

"He spoke out plainly to those spies of Herod who came to try to trap him into saying something they could call a sin. They have gone away angry. Even some of those who were his friends have now left him." Simeon shook his head. "They do not want a Kingdom of Heaven, they want a kingdom of Israel."

"I will never leave Jesus," said Nathan, sitting up suddenly, "because I belong to his Kingdom."

Anna gently eased Enoch from her shoulder, where he had dropped to sleep, and put him down on the mat. Then she said to Nathan: "Would you like to tell us what you did this afternoon, my son?"

So Nathan told his story. He didn't make very much of having stood up for Eber, because it seemed as though any friend would have done the same. But Anna and Simeon did not think it was a small thing, and Renah leaned forward to slip her arm around Nathan's shoulders. When he had finished, Simeon looked at Anna and smiled, but he only said: "I think we need not be ashamed of our son, Anna."

Anna said nothing, but Nathan could read the pride and love in her dark eyes. He looked at his father, browned by the sun and strong from ploughing and reaping — a man any son would be proud of. He put his hand on Renah's arm, and felt the little curls of her hair against his cheek. His eyes went to Enoch, still scarcely more than a baby, and turned again to his mother on whose face the Passover moon had cast an almost holy light. And it came to Nathan that here, right here in his own home, was the Kingdom of Heaven, because they loved each other so much.

Chapter x

THE HOLY CITY

"We go up to Jerusalem"

NATHAN and Enoch were on their knees watching a dove which had fluttered into the courtyard of their home. The bird stood for an instant with its feathers puffed out and one leg drawn up, while its open beak showed it was fighting for breath.

"It is sick," said Nathan, putting out his hand to touch the dove. At his movement the dove put down its other foot and wobbled weakly around the courtyard.

"It acts like I did before Jesus made my legs well," said Enoch. "Do you think we could take the bird to Jesus to be healed, Nathan?"

Anna got up from the mill where she and Renah were

grinding the grain into flour for the day's baking. She gently captured the sick bird and held it in her hands where it seemed to feel her kindness and was quiet, although its breast feathers still showed how fast its heart was beating.

"I think the dove has escaped from someone's basket," said Anna. "Perhaps one of the pilgrims going to Jerusalem for the Feast of Passover has lost part of the offering he had planned for the altar in the Temple. It may be sick or only frightened, but you must not take the bird to Jesus, Enoch. Too many people run to him for things they might do themselves. He loves all little creatures, but the work he has to do is to heal the hearts of men and make them strong." Anna looked down at the bird in her hands and a shadow came over her face. She spoke softly and only Nathan heard her say, "There may be so little time." The words gave Nathan a sudden chill of fear.

"What shall we do with it, Mother?" asked Enoch anxiously.

"We will put it in a quiet corner," said Anna, "and you can give it some food and water. Then we shall see whether it is really hurt or only frightened. I think, Enoch, we may be able to cure the dove ourselves."

While they were making the bird comfortable, Juda and Eber came running down the street. Nathan left the care of the dove to his mother and Enoch and went to meet them. Eber brought good news. His father had arranged with the rabbi for him to go to the synagogue school. He would start today. The boys would not be mean to him again because Jared had said so. Nathan was glad to hear this for he had been feeling more and more that he and Eber would be good friends.

Juda also brought news, but Nathan did not feel as happy about Juda's news as he had about Eber's. "Jesus is going away," said Juda, "and my father and the rest of the twelve disciples are going with him."

"Are they going to Jerusalem for the Feast of Passover?" asked Nathan, feeling again that chill of fear.

Anna, leaving Renah to help Enoch with the dove, came over to see if Juda had brought any message from his mother. She heard what they were saying, and waited for Juda to answer Nathan's question.

"No," said Juda, "I think they are going the other way, to the northwest. They did not go by the lake shore. But no one knows where they will go."

Anna drew a quick breath and Nathan felt his body grow warm again. But a thought, which he had once before brushed away like a troublesome insect, crept again into his mind. He felt ashamed and unhappy but it was there. Suppose Jesus were running away from this danger which the older people seemed to fear for him. Suppose he should never come back this way. A longing to see him again swept through Nathan and he wondered if he ran out to the hills and climbed to the top of the highest one he could still see Jesus and his friends before they were out of sight. He asked his mother if he and Juda and Eber might do this, and Anna said they might if they would be back in time for school.

It did not take long to get out of the city, and then they turned off into the fields and followed sheep tracks up into the hills. This was the kind of day when Nathan would have loved to go slowly and hunt out all the little hidden pools, and the wooded places where early spring would have some surprises ready, but now he wanted only to reach a hilltop where he could look off to the north and west. He remembered that it was not far from this spot that he had seen Jesus the first time. The boys stopped for breath and Nathan looked around. Yes, there was the very rock behind which he had hidden when he was listening to Jesus speaking to Peter and Andrew and the rest of his friends, nearly a year ago.

Juda and Eber were looking around, too, and it was Eber who first saw the Twelve with their Master. "Look!" he cried.

They were coming along the ridge of the hill. The sunlight was warm on their faces and the wind rippled the tunics about their strong brown legs as they strode along. They passed not far from where the boys were standing but did not see them. Their eyes were on the far hills toward which they were journeying. Then Nathan scrambled up the slope and ran after them. He put out his hand and just touched the edge of Jesus's tunic. "Master," he whispered, "will you come back?"

Jesus looked down, and it seemed to Nathan that look went deep into his heart and saw what was there. "I will always come back, Nathan," said Jesus with a smile. Nathan did not know until much later how full of meaning the words were, but he knew all his unhappiness and doubt were gone.

The Holy City

When Juda and Eber caught up with Nathan, Jesus and the Twelve had gone on. The three boys stood watching them until they passed out of sight. Ahead lay the long, winding way that led to the shores of the Great Sea. Nathan had often seen camel caravans come across these hill roads, bringing goods to sell in Capernaum. The merchants came from Tyre and Sidon, cities on the Great Sea which were ports where ships from every nation bordering on that sea gathered. They were strange-looking people, Nathan always thought, so different from his own race. His father had told him they were fearless sailors, not afraid to voyage to far-distant places to trade and to bring back other goods.

"Do you think they are going as far as Tyre and Sidon?" Nathan asked Juda and Eber.

The boys drew in their breath at the idea of such an adventure. "They might," said Juda, and his eyes were big with the thought of Peter, Andrew, James, and John, fishermen of the Sea of Galilee, in the cities on the shore of that much vaster sea.

Off in the distance now, Jesus and the Twelve had reached the top of a hill from which the way went downward until it started to climb the rocky hills beyond, too far for the eye to follow. Soon they would pass out of sight. For a moment the boys could see them against the blue of the sky, and it seemed to Nathan that the wide world lay at their feet. Then they were gone, and the boys raced back to the city for fear they would be late at the synagogue school and be scolded by the rabbi.

That spring was a busy time for Nathan. His father let

him help on the farm with the barley and wheat harvests. He was bigger and stronger than the year before, so after his lessons at the synagogue he would go out to the fields and join with the other helpers in loading the donkeys with bundles of cut grain, which they carried to the threshing floor. Simeon let Nathan have one of the donkeys for his own use, and laughed when he saw how the little animal would not work for any one else when Nathan was around. Nathan liked to rub his cheek against the soft places on the donkey's nose and pull his long ears, or run his hand along the shaggy flank while he piled the sheaves of sweet-smelling barley or wheat on his back. It made him feel they were working together as partners, and it seemed as though the donkey felt this, too, and carried his load much more willingly.

One night, during the wheat harvest, Simeon let Nathan stay all night at the farm. He ate, with his father and the other men, the supper which Renah had brought to them, while he exulted in the way the hot sun was giving his skin an extra coat of brown, and felt the evening wind cool on his body . . . wind which blew down from Mount Hermon after the sun had set. Joseph was there, and Asa. Nathan had not seen Joseph to speak to since that day on the hillside when he and his friends had wanted to make Jesus king of Israel. Joseph had been working on the farm but he had been quiet — as though there was something in his mind that troubled him, thought Nathan. The old Joseph had been noisy about his work, sometimes teasing the children in the fields, or having a cheerful word with

148

the women and girls who gathered what was left after the men had cut and bound up the grain.

Asa was always the same. Nathan thought there was a stillness about him like the hills, or like growing things that had a secret understanding with the earth and ran no chance of turning into something different any day or season. Whatever happened to Asa, Nathan felt sure, would happen inside, and would show only in the kindness of his eyes which wrinkled around the corners when he smiled, or by the gentle but sure way he went about his work. Asa talked to the oxen as he fastened them to the threshing cart or led them away to pasture at night. He handled the yoke lovingly as he laid it on their necks or took it off. He told Nathan that Jesus had showed the carpenter of Capernaum how to make the yokes smooth and easy for the necks of the oxen. Jesus had learned the trade in Nazareth as a boy. Asa and the oxen seemed to understand each other.

When supper had been eaten, they lay back against a big pile of straw and Asa and Simeon talked for a while of the crops and tried to decide whether they were better this year than usual. Later all would wrap their cloaks around them and lie down to sleep, excepting the one whose duty it was to see that robbers did not creep in and steal the ripe grain. But first there was the long twilight with the sun still painting the crown of Mount Hermon pink, although it had disappeared behind the near-by hills and left the farm in shadow.

Nathan lay on his back and listened to the voices of the men while the muscles of his arms and legs little by little lost their tired ache. He thought he felt more comfortable now than if there had never been an ache. He was looking at Mount Hermon, soft gray with a rosy top, and thinking about the world that stretched beyond the mountains. Nathan did not know much about those far countries except what he learned from the travelers who came through Capernaum, like the merchant princes from the East, or the traders from the Great Sea, or the Arabs from beyond Judea.

Wondering about these places made Nathan think of that morning when he had seen Jesus and his friends start on their journey toward the Great Sea. That had been before the Feast of Passover and it was now nearly time for the Feast of Pentecost, which came after the wheat crops had been harvested. He wondered where they had been, and what they had been doing among these people who were not at all like the people of Galilee or Judea. Nathan had a feeling that it would not matter to Jesus how different they were, because the Kingdom of Heaven was not a kingdom of Israel. It had room in it for the whole world. Would Jesus be king of the whole world? Nathan's heart leaped at the thought. Then he asked himself: Could the Prince of Peace be a king?

Joseph moved closer to Nathan as though he had read his thoughts. "I heard something about your 'Prince of Peace' today, Nathan," he said in a low voice so only Nathan could hear.

Nathan thought he sounded as though he were teasing him and he squirmed a little, because it hurt to have Joseph speak of Jesus as the Prince of Peace in that way. But he sat up and listened eagerly as Joseph went on: "One of the gleaners comes from Bethsaida. She had a blind brother. Well — Jesus was there, and the brother is no longer blind."

"Is Jesus coming back to Capernaum?" Nathan asked, his eyes bright and his breath coming hard.

"I don't know," said Joseph, chewing on a piece of straw and looking, Nathan thought, unhappy and out of patience with someone — perhaps himself. "No one knows what he will do. But wherever he goes he takes the crowd with him." Joseph's eyes suddenly had a gleam in them and he got up and walked off into the shadows.

Nathan looked at his father and Asa. They were still talking about the crops, so he fell back again on the straw and watched the shadows spread and the stars come out, while he kept warm in his heart the glad news that Jesus was again in Galilee. Later he would tell Simeon and Asa. They would be happy, too. And tomorrow he would run to Peter's house. Perhaps — oh, there were so many wonderful things that might happen if he found Jesus there! Nathan dreamed on until the stars were thick in the heavens, making him think, as they so often did, of the song in The Book of Praise about the heavens telling of the glory of God. Then he rolled over and fell asleep.

But Nathan was not to see Jesus the next day, nor for many days. It was believed he had gone to Jerusalem for the Feast of Pentecost. Nathan heard his mother and father talk softly together, and there were other times during the summer when Jesus's friends, meeting in Simeon's house, spoke in a worried way about his travels. Then, in the early autumn, when the vineyards and orchards were again heavy with fruit and the time of the Feast of Tabernacles, or Booths, was near, Juda told Nathan a message from Peter had come, telling Sara that they were in Galilee once more. The two boys talked excitedly about this news.

"Perhaps," said Juda, "they will come to Capernaum for the Feast."

"Jesus might even go out to the hillside where we have our booths," cried Nathan, thinking how hard he would work to make them more beautiful than usual.

"He will see how strong we have grown, Nathan," said Juda proudly, "when we carry the big baskets of grapes and olives."

"Yes," agreed Nathan with flushed cheeks. "And, Juda, he might be in the synagogue when we offer our first fruits to God." It came to Nathan that God would seem much closer if Jesus were in the synagogue, that more than the fruit would be lifted up. Their hearts would go singing up almost out of their bodies with joy. Nathan had felt that so often when Jesus was near.

The hopes of the boys and many other friends were dashed, for Jesus did not come to Capernaum for the feast. Later, when some of those who had gone to celebrate the harvest feast in Jerusalem came home, they said he had been in the Temple, teaching. They said that Caiaphas, the High Priest of the temple, had sent his officers to arrest Jesus but they did not do it. They had listened to what he was saying and were afraid to arrest such a good man.

The Holy City

Listening to his mother and father talking about this report, Nathan felt very proud. Jesus was not afraid to go to Jerusalem and teach in the Temple. It was his enemies who were afraid. Perhaps they might even come to love him. How could they help it when they understood about the Kingdom? Then Jesus could come and go to Jerusalem without his friends being so full of fear that something dreadful might happen to him.

Just before the early autumn rains began, Jesus really was back in Capernaum. He was in Peter's house and Nathan knew once more the joy of finding him there sometimes when he went home with Juda or took a message from his mother to Sara.

"You are so willing to take my messages to Sara, Nathan," said Anna, teasing him one day. "The words are hardly out of my mouth before you are off. Take Enoch with you to remind you not to stay too long. I do not want you to be in danger of making yourself a nuisance. There," she added as she saw the hurt look on Nathan's face, "I know you do not, my son, for Sara tells me you never put yourself forward. But remember never to let your love for Jesus get in his way."

Enoch, having heard his mother's suggestion that he should go along, came running to join Nathan and they went off, Nathan a little sobered by what his mother had said. When they reached Peter's house they found Sara sitting by the door with her spinning. Juda, she said, had run down to the shore for some fish. From inside came the voices of men, some of them raised as though they were almost angry, thought Nathan in surprise. As they were talking with Sara, Jesus came to the doorway. His face was a little sad and he looked as though the voices of the men inside had tired him. He smiled when he saw Nathan and Enoch. Turning toward the room inside, he called his followers to him.

"See," said Jesus, sitting down and drawing Enoch to his knee, "you talk among yourselves about who shall be called the greatest of my disciples. Whoever receives this little child in my name receives me, and whoever receives me receives Him that sent me. For it is the lowliest of you who is great."

The men were quiet now. They seemed to understand what Jesus had been saying. Then John spoke about something that had happened in the city and Jesus went back inside the house with them.

As Nathan and Enoch were running down to the shore to join Juda, Enoch wanted to know what Jesus had said about him. Nathan had been thinking about that. It was not entirely clear to him, but he felt that Jesus had meant to make plain to his friends that it was not the one who thought he deserved to be called great who should be the chief of his disciples, but the one who felt the least important — like a little child who didn't expect to be first in anything — or like Asa who was gentle and satisfied with the good earth which God had given him for his use and asked for nothing better. "Enoch," said Nathan, slowing down to a walk, "Jesus said you were important to him He made you a lesson to the disciples! But," he added in warning, "you mustn't think so, or — you will not be."

Enoch's eyes were round with excitement. He had lost the warning and remembered only that he was important to Jesus. "Did he say that, Nathan?" he asked in wonder, "*Did* he?"

Winter had not yet come when Jesus and the Twelve were gone again. This time, Nathan heard Simeon tell Anna, it was probable they would be in Jerusalem for the mid-winter festival which celebrated the return of the Temple to the Jewish people after it had been in the hands of their enemies. This festival was called the Feast of Lights. It would be a wonderful time to be in Jerusalem, thought Nathan, his mind afire with the memory of the story of Judas Maccabeus, a great national hero of the Jews because he had restored their temple to them. It was right for Jesus to be there at this time. Nathan had lost his fear about Jerusalem. Jesus seemed to come and go as he wished and no one dared to take him. They would talk of him when they lighted the candles in their own home for the feast, and think of that greater celebration in Jerusalem. Perhaps in the spring, thought Nathan, his father would think he was old enough to go for the Feast of the Passover. Simeon had said no more about it, but Nathan resolved that he would work hard at his lessons, and he hoped he would grow fast for the next few months. Then, perhaps, his father would feel he was not too young to go to Jerusalem at twelve years instead of thirteen.

So the months passed and the winter rains had once more washed the face of the earth until it was cleansed of all the old year's dust and stain, and spring was making it rosy with scarlet anemones. On Nathan's twelfth birthday, Simeon measured Nathan against his shoulder. "See, Anna," he said, "the top of his head reaches my shoulder now. I think I shall take him to Jerusalem this year for the Feast of Passover."

Nathan felt very still inside and it was hard to keep the tears from coming into his eyes as he looked up at his father. This was the moment he had longed for and the happiness almost hurt. Simeon was looking at Anna so Nathan, also, turned toward his mother.

Anna's face was thoughtful and she poured a little water from the jar into a basin of flour, in which she was mixing some cakes for Nathan's birthday, before she answered. "Some people think there may be trouble in Jerusalem this year, Simeon. I have heard Jairus speak of it."

What trouble, Nathan wondered, his face falling and the old fear catching at his throat. He waited to hear what his father would say.

"If there should be trouble," answered Simeon, "he will need his friends. Yes, we will go, Anna, you and I and Nathan. He can take the long journey now on foot, and you shall have one of the donkeys to ride. Renah shall stay here with Enoch and they can eat the Passover supper with our cousins.

"He will need his friends." That could mean only one thing, thought Nathan. Jesus would go to the feast. And he, Nathan, would be counted as one of his friends. He would stand by him, just as he had stood by Eber, if there was any trouble. But there would be no trouble because people had only to listen to Jesus to love him. Wouldn't it be wonderful to have Jesus there when he first went to the Temple? Nathan's thoughts raced along and his heart lifted again.

Anna was saying: "Then we must make our plans to start with the caravan which will be going in about two weeks." She looked at Nathan with a smile as though she had just realized that he was waiting for her to be glad with him that the journey he had looked forward to so long was really to come this year. "I shall be proud to take our tall son to Jerusalem," she said, and Nathan felt his cup of joy was full.

When Sara, Simon Peter's wife, heard that Anna and Simeon were taking Nathan to Jerusalem for the feast, she decided to go and take Juda. She knew that Peter would be with Jesus and the rest of the disciples if they were there. Sara had not heard from Peter for many weeks although it was known that Jesus and the Twelve had been in the hills to the south, in the region of some beautiful cities built by the Greek people. Some of the families of the disciples had gone to join them there. Simeon said Sara might take one of his donkeys to ride on, so the two families made their preparations, and Nathan and Juda could hardly wait for the day to arrive.

It came at last! A day of warm sunshine and blue skies. Nathan had been sleeping on the roof top and his eyes flew open when the first rays of the sun fell across his face. He knew there would be no time this morning to idle and dream, as he sometimes did, until his mother had to call him from the courtyard more than once before he could rouse himself. Nathan did not know whether the sun had awakened him or the bray of a donkey in the street below. He jumped up and looked over the edge of the roof. Simeon was loading the last things on the backs of two donkeys. Sara and Juda had come over the night before to bring their bags of food and other things necessary for the journey. Simeon was now arranging mats as saddles on the donkeys so Sara and Anna could ride comfortably. Nathan felt sorry that he had not gone down early enough to help. He ran down the stairs in a hurry and was followed by Enoch who had been awakened by Nathan's moving around. Enoch cried a little because he was not going, too, but his mother comforted him with the thought that his time would surely come. Renah bustled about, helping Anna. Girls did not feel the same way about going to Jerusalem as boys did, thought Nathan. Renah felt important to be in charge of the home while her mother was away. Some day she would have her own son to take up to the feast.

Sara and Juda came before they had finished eating breakfast, and soon they were all ready to start. Anna's donkey put his nose in Nathan's hand to beg for a last crumb, which he seemed sure Nathan was hiding there. It was the donkey that had been Nathan's in the wheat fields and they knew each other's habits. Simeon had chosen him because he wanted Nathan to lead him, and he knew he would follow willingly. Now they were off, with Enoch watching them out of sight and waving his hand as long as they could see him.

The Holy City

In the market place they joined other travelers and made quite a large caravan as they started out of the city and along the curving shore of the lake southward. It was the same way Nathan and Juda had taken that morning, more than a year ago, when they had gone to spend the day with Benjamin, the shepherd. The caravan was long, although not all of the people who were planning to go to Jerusalem for the feast were starting so early. Many who, like Simeon and Anna, had kinsfolk in or near the city and expected to spend a whole week in Jerusalem, were leaving a few days ahead of the rest. Other caravans would be starting every day as long as they could reach Jerusalem in time to eat the Passover supper. Nathan was surprised to see Joseph and some of the young men who had been in the boat that day he had gone with them across the lake. They kept together and were at the head of the caravan when it started from the market place. There was another surprise when Nathan discovered Eber with his mother and the rest of Matthew's family. Like Sara, who hoped to see Peter, they hoped that Matthew would be in Jerusalem with Jesus.

It was a long journey for the boys, more than eighty miles, over the hills of Galilee and along the Jordan River valley until they reached the final climb up the rough Judean hills to Jerusalem. It would take three days, but the boys were full of excitement and eager to start. They had to set their pace to that of the caravan which moved slowly, and it seemed to Nathan as though, at this rate, they would never get anywhere. But after a while he was happy just to be walking at the head of his mother's donkey, in the full

glory of the springtime, along the road which led past Magdala and across the lovely Plain of Genessaret where groves of walnut and olive trees made pleasant shade in the middle of the day, and where nearly every flower and vine was already in bloom. Anna was singing softly a song of her people:

> "For, lo, the winter is past,
> The rain is over and gone;
> The flowers appear on the earth,
> The time of the singing of birds is come."

Food tasted good when they stopped to rest, and at night, when they made their camp under the stars, Nathan and the other boys were so tired and sleepy that they rolled up in their cloaks and were fast asleep before they knew it.

Toward sunset on the second day of their journey, the caravan came in sight of the city of Jericho. Simeon planned to camp on the outskirts of this beautiful city which Herod the Great, king of Israel, had built, and in which he had lived in the wintertime when Jerusalem was too cold. They could see his marble palace and other great buildings set in gardens and palm trees. It was a refreshing sight after the heat of the Jordan valley through which they had been travelling all day. Some Pilgrims went through Samaria, which was a pleasanter way to travel to Jerusalem than the way Nathan's caravan had come, but the Samaritans did not show much friendliness to these travelers. They believed that God should be worshiped on their mountain, Mount Gerizim, and not on Mount Zion where Jerusalem had been built. So Simeon had chosen the way which would avoid any disputes or quarrels with the people of Samaria. He had planned, also, to reach Jericho just before the Jewish Sabbath so there would be a day to rest and get ready for the last day of their journey when they would have the hardest climb of all ahead of them.

Many caravan routes came together at Jericho, so Pilgrims were crowding into the city from every direction. Nathan felt a little frightened by the press of people with their camel and donkey trains. He was happier when his father found the place he was looking for in a grove outside the city. Here, with Sara and Juda and Matthew's family, they prepared to camp until the Sabbath was over, for the Jews did not travel on the Sabbath. Most of the caravan from Capernaum had gone on into the city, and, looking around from the top of the hill where they had made their camp, Nathan could see the roads to the north, east, and west were full of travelers.

Simeon pointed out to Nathan, Juda, and Eber the hills of Gilead and showed them the way Moses had brought the children of Israel from the desert to Mount Nebo, where they could see the land which God had promised them. That was where Moses had died, Simeon told them, and then Joshua had led the Israelites across the Jordan to capture Jericho. The boys knew the story well, but it made their eyes bulge to think that right at this spot, perhaps, their forefathers had camped before taking the city.

Half an hour before sunset the sound of three trumpet blasts reached them from the city. This was the signal that the Sabbath would begin with the setting of the sun. In Jewish families the men went to the synagogue for a Sabbath evening service, so Simeon left them and went in to Jericho. He did not return as soon as they expected, so Anna said the Sabbath prayer, and poured the water from the jar that they might cleanse their hands and feel clean both outwardly and inwardly. These were the simple Sabbath rites that no Jew forgot to perform. Then they all sat down and ate their supper.

The boys were tired, and their mothers wanted them to go to sleep early, so they tried to obey. Nathan lay face downward with his head buried in his arms so his eyes would stay shut, but his thoughts were still busy. He wondered why his father had not come back, and whether, in all these crowds, Jesus and the Twelve might not be traveling to Jerusalem. Suppose they should meet on the road, and Jesus should lead them into the Holy City. People would be sure then to crown him their king and put him on the throne of David! Young men like Joseph would want to put a sword in his hand and legions of soldiers at his back and go out with him to destroy and drive the Romans from their land. But that — Nathan laughed under his breath — that was such a false picture of Jesus. That would not be Jesus at all. He did not destroy men. He made them well and happy.

Nathan turned on his side and opened his eyes. He saw the lamps being lighted in the windows of the city, a little warm glow in homes where people ate their Sabbath suppers and said their prayers. The air was sweet from orchards where a kind of bush grew which was used to make a rare perfume.

Nathan sniffed it with pleasure and finally drifted off to sleep.

When morning came, swiftly and suddenly as it always did with the sunrise, Nathan reached out to pull his cloak over his face to keep the bright sunlight from his eyes until they should be able to bear it. Then he remembered that his father had not come back the night before while he was awake, so he threw off the cover and sat up.

Not far away Juda and Eber were still sleeping, but farther on, in a little grove of trees, Nathan could see the older people sitting. His father was there, and he was talking to Anna and Sara and Matthew's wife, Leah. There was also Eber's older sister with her husband. They were taking their baby to be presented in the Temple according to the Jewish custom. The baby was sleeping near by. Nathan got up and went over to join them. He sat down quietly by his mother. The others were listening too intently to Simeon to notice him. Nathan thought their faces looked tired as though they had not slept.

"So," Simeon was saying, "he is going to Jerusalem to face his enemies, and that will give them an opportunity to take him. In Jericho there is great excitement. Many will follow him to Jerusalem, but some are angry because he is spending the Sabbath at the home of Zacchaeus, a man who has made money from their taxes, and who, they say, is a great sinner. I have heard from others that Zacchaeus has promised to give all his money to the poor, and to return to those he has cheated four times as much, but most of the pilgrims are not pleased." Simeon shook his head.

The Holy City

"Who but the Master would be fearless enough to give his enemies an excuse for another charge against him?"

Nathan put his face close to his mother's ear. "Is Jesus in Jericho, mother?" he whispered, although he knew the answer.

Anna put her arm around him. "Yes, my son," she said.

Simeon heard their voices and saw Nathan for the first time. He looked at him thoughtfully. "Yes, Nathan," he said at last, "Jesus is in Jericho, but we shall not go into the city today. We will keep the Sabbath quietly here, and tomorrow we will start early and join the company of Jesus's friends who will go with him to Jerusalem."

Nathan wanted to ask more questions but his father seemed in a strange mood. One thing was clear. Jesus was going to stand up and face his enemies and Nathan felt he knew who would come out first. Had not Jesus been to all the feasts lately and no one had hurt him?

Nathan tried to smother a little spark of fear that suddenly kindled in his heart when he looked at the serious faces around him. Then he jumped up and ran to awaken Juda and Eber with the news about tomorrow. The most wonderful thing he had hoped would happen was going to happen. They would follow Jesus up the steep ascent to the Holy City, Jerusalem. Nathan thought it would be the happiest day of his life.

Chapter xi

THE KING OF LOVE

"I lay down my life to take it up again"

BEFORE daybreak the next morning, the donkeys were loaded and the mats thrown across their backs for the women to ride upon. The sun was not yet up when the little party went through Jericho. Simeon had seen Matthew and he had told him where they could join the company of Jesus's closest friends, some of whom had come a long way with Jesus and the twelve disciples. The city was stirring and soon the crowds would be pouring out of the gates going toward Jerusalem.

Simeon stopped and drew to one side of the road just beyond the gates of the city. Nathan watched the dawn flash across the hills and light up the roofs of the buildings. It touched first the fortress which overlooked the town, then warmed the marble of the palace and the amphitheatre where Roman games and sports were held. Jericho was ruled by the Roman governor, Pontius Pilate, Simeon told him. Nathan liked it best when the sun had reached the palm trees and orchards, and brought out the colors of the fruit and flowers. Pilgrims began to pass them and Nathan watched longingly for the face he loved.

At last they came, Jesus and the Twelve who had been his closest companions for so many months. They seemed to walk apart although they were followed by a multitude that reached as far as the eye could see. To Nathan, Jesus walked alone and he started forward as though to grasp his tunic, but Anna leaned down from her donkey and caught his arm, holding him back while Simeon led his party into an opening in the crowd which some friends from Capernaum made for them.

In that moment, Nathan had seen a look on Jesus's face which was new and strange to him. He felt that Jesus did not see the flowers he loved by the roadside, or the birds that flew into the air with frightened cries as they passed along, or even a fox which sprang out of the bushes and disappeared across the road just ahead. He did not seem to see the road or the people that pressed around him. He did not see Nathan or the rest of his friends. His eyes were looking ahead, not at the bleak hills of Judea which they must climb, but far, far beyond. It seemed to Nathan in that moment when he had gazed at his face, that Jesus looked as though he saw a city no one else could see, and that he had set his feet on the road to that city, and no man might turn him back. But, of course, Nathan thought as he hurried along at the head of his mother's donkey, Jesus was going to Jerusalem. What other city could there be?

The crowd was excited. This was the last day of their journey. One man cried out: "This is the 'son of David.' This is the king who will save Israel." Nathan thought the man's voice sounded like Joseph's. The crowd took up the cry, and as they moved all day up the steep, winding road, the voices joined in singing some of the familiar songs which pilgrims used on this final stage of their journey. Nathan knew these songs, so did Juda and Eber. They had learned them in the synagogue school. They sang with the others:

> "I was glad when they said unto me,
> 'Let us go into the house of the Lord.'
> Our feet shall stand within thy gates,
> O Jerusalem.
>
> .   .   .   .
>
> Peace be within thy walls,
> And prosperity within thy palaces,
> For my brothers' and my companions' sake,
> I will now say, 'Peace be within thee.' "

The King of Love

The hills echoed their songs, and the joy of the words filled their hearts.

It was afternoon when Nathan saw two of the disciples leave the road and cross the fields to a little village which was farther up the side of the hill they were climbing. This hill was the Mount of Olives and there was a lovely town called Bethany near by where Jesus had some very dear friends. Nathan thought Jesus might be going to stop there, but he continued to move on. It seemed only a few moments before the disciples who had gone off were back, leading a donkey with the prettiest little colt Nathan had ever seen running beside her. Some of the other disciples had their cloaks ready to throw across the back of the donkey and Jesus seated himself on them. A great shout rose from the crowd. Most of the people knew what the Scroll of the prophet Zachariah said. Nathan heard his father repeating it now, and he looked up into his face. Simeon was chanting:

> "Rejoice, greatly, O daughter of Zion;
> Shout, O daughter of Jerusalem:
> Behold thy King cometh unto thee:
> He is just and having salvation.
> Lowly he comes, riding upon an ass,
> Even upon a colt, the foal of an ass."

Nathan's eyes were shining. The words, "thy King cometh unto thee," rang in his ears. Was Jesus really going to let them make him a king? Would they crown him the "son of David" in David's city? All the hopes and longings of his people for a Messiah, one who should save them, were in Nathan's heart at that moment. Men and boys were strip-

ping the palm trees. Simeon took the bridle of Anna's
donkey from Nathan's hand and let him run with Juda and
Eber to join them. They waved the palm branches and cried
"Hosanna! Hosanna!" while Joseph and some of the others
tore off their cloaks and threw them down for Jesus to ride
over. Never, it seemed to Nathan, had there been such joy.

Shouting and singing, they came at last to a place where
the city of Jerusalem was in sight. It rose high and beautiful
above a deep ravine which they had still to cross. The great
white stone towers and buildings shone in the light of the
setting sun, while the golden roof of the Temple seemed to
have gathered every lingering ray to itself. Under that roof,
Nathan knew, was the Sacred Rock on which Abraham had
been willing to offer his son, Isaac, as a sacrifice if God had
wished it. Nathan was glad God had not let Abraham do
this dreadful thing. And under that temple roof, also, had
been placed the Ark of the Covenant which the Israelites
had carried so many years on their journeys through the
desert. Abraham, Moses, David — the great figures of his
people's history raced through Nathan's mind.

He pushed his way to the edge of the crowd and gazed
in awe. Then, suddenly, he felt a soft nose in his hand. He
turned and saw that the little colt of the donkey which
Jesus rode was pressing against him. Nathan rubbed its head
and looked up at the people near him. Just a few steps
away, Jesus and the Twelve had stopped and were also
looking across the ravine at the Holy City. Nathan's eyes
went from face to face. He had again the feeling that Jesus
was seeing something that no one else could see. His face

was stern. He looks, thought Nathan, as though he were crying inside. Then the multitude surged forward down into the ravine and up the other side. Their shouts brought the people of Jerusalem out to meet them. As they swept through the city gates, Nathan felt his father's hand on his shoulder.

"We will turn aside here, my son," said Simeon. "Your mother is tired and we will not follow the crowd to the Temple tonight. We will go to the house of your uncle, Obed ben Eli, and rest."

Nathan was glad to lie down on his sleeping mat that night. His legs were aching from the strain of the long climb, and his thoughts had been troubled by that strange, new look on Jesus's face. Now that the excitement was over, Nathan felt sure Jesus would never let his followers try to make him the kind of king most of them wanted. What would happen? Nathan had seen Roman soldiers in the streets on the way to his uncle's house. He had seen, too, groups of men talking together who did not seem pleased with the multitude which had followed Jesus into the city. Nathan wondered whether Jesus and this great company of pilgrims had gone at once to the temple. He wished his father had let him go all the way with them, although there had been moments when the pushing and shouting of the crowd had been a little terrifying. He wondered if Juda and Eber had gone on with the rest, or whether they, too, had been taken by their families to the places where they would stay while in Jerusalem. Nathan could hear his father and uncle talking together in low tones on the roof top outside the guest room, which he with his mother and father would occupy while they were Obed's guests. The sound of their voices was still in his ears when he finally fell asleep.

Simeon had promised to take Nathan to the temple the next morning, although the Passover sacrifice would not be offered at the great altar for several days. Simeon knew it would be hard for Nathan to wait so long to see the wonders of the Temple about which he had dreamed so many months. He smiled when he saw the boy's eyes begging him almost as soon as they were open, and he nodded to show they would not be long in starting.

Anna went with them and as they climbed up the hilly, winding streets toward the Temple, the press of pilgrims, who were already pouring into the city, became greater and greater. Bazaars were doing a thriving business with pilgrims who had come from every part of the Roman Empire, which extended far to the north, east, south, and west of Jerusalem. The Jewish people had scattered and settled in all parts of the world, but they turned to Jerusalem, if they possibly could, at the Passover season. This was a profitable time of the year for merchants and they were making the most of it. Anna stopped to buy a little cheese and some fresh dates so her family would not be a burden to their host, and Nathan saw a toy which he wanted to take to Enoch. In another bazaar, he found a pretty necklace for Renah.

The sun was high when they passed through the gates that led into the outer courts of the Temple. Nathan caught his breath as he found himself in a vast enclosure, with tall marble pillars holding up a roof that seemed miles high.

He wanted to close his eyes an instant. Simeon laughed and told him that this colonnade went around all sides of the Temple. It was called the Court of the Gentiles, because people of all nations and every race could come into it. That was nice, thought Nathan, for everybody to worship God together. Jesus would like that. Farther on, Simeon was explaining, they would come to a screen beyond which none but Jews were allowed to go. There was a Stone of Forbidding that gave notice to foreigners that they might not enter the inner courts.

"On the day of the feast," said Simeon, "we shall go through the Gate Beautiful into the Court of Women. The gate is so immense, Nathan, that it takes twenty men to open it in the morning and close it at night. The Court of Women is as far as you and your mother may go. Beyond that is the Court of Priests where only the priests and Jewish men who wish to sacrifice may enter. In the Court of Priests is the altar and the Holy of Holies, which is over the Sacred Rock and is hidden by a curtain."

After his first awe and amazement at the size of the Court of the Gentiles, and the thought of the still greater marvels he was to see, Nathan became aware of a terrible noise and confusion of voices mingled with the cries of animals. His ears had been so full of the sounds of the bazaars and other unusual city noises that he had not noticed this at once. He asked his father what it was, but, before Simeon could answer, they had reached a place from which Nathan could see a strange sight.

Droves of calves and lambs had been brought by their

owners to the Court of the Gentiles to be sold to the pilgrims for their Passover sacrifices. There were thousands of doves, too. And in the midst of all these animals were tables with piles of money on them. Men at the tables, Simeon said, were changing the money of the pilgrims who came from other places into the only kind of coins the Temple would accept. Each pilgrim, excepting women and children, had also a tax to pay, so there was a great deal of money changing hands. Even Nathan knew that a large amount of cheating went on at times like these.

Pilgrims, who had finished with the money-changers, were pushing around among the animals to select a perfect one for sacrifice. Voices were raised in angry protest at some sharp bargains that had been forced upon them, and, as Nathan and his parents drew near enough to take in the whole picture, the din was so deafening that Nathan wanted to cover his ears. He felt like closing his eyes, too, but he could only clutch his father's hand and stare at this most unbelievable sight. He knew that young animals were killed and used as sacrifices in the Temple, and he had seen doves caught at Magdala and carried off on donkeys to be sold in Jerusalem, but here, in such numbers, their frightened cries brought a tight feeling in his throat.

He thought of Benjamin who could not rest until he had found the one little lamb that was lost. He remembered the lame dove which had escaped and flown into their courtyard a year ago. Anna had cured it and it was Enoch's very dear pet. Did God really like to be worshiped with the blood of animals, Nathan wondered? This was a daring question to have come into his mind, because Nathan had been brought up to believe all the Jewish customs were sacred and dear to God.

A man at one of the tables was taking too much money from a poor peasant who was complaining bitterly about it. Their voices rose in shrill cries. Nathan wondered if, in the Holy of Holies where God's presence was believed to be always close to his people, God could hear what was going on. Only priests might enter that holy place, yet it was not far from all this dishonesty and confusion. Nathan looked at his father in fear and Simeon returned his gaze sadly. This was where he, himself, would buy his lamb before he entered the Court of Priests to kill it and make his Passover sacrifice on the Great Altar. His lips moved and Nathan took his fingers out of his ears so he could hear what his father was saying. The words were from the Scroll of the prophet Isaiah. Nathan had heard them read many times in the synagogue at Capernaum. "My house shall be called a house of prayer for all people," Simeon was quoting.

Suddenly there was the crash of a table overturned, and the tinkling of coins on the stone floor. Money-changers and tax collectors scrambled after them, and the frightened animals stampeded for the gates, upsetting other tables as they ran. Simeon pulled Anna and Nathan behind one of the big pillars where they would not be crushed in the excitement that followed. Then, above the noise, a voice was heard. It was like a great echo of the words which Simeon had spoken. Nathan knew it was the voice of Jesus even before he caught sight of him standing not far away with his little group of disciples, but he had never heard this sound — like the cutting of a whip — in that voice before. Nathan thought Jesus's face was both wonderful and frightening. It made him think of the sudden storms that sometimes broke in a fury over the Sea of Galilee. "It is written," cried Jesus, " 'My house shall be called a house of prayer.' " Then he added: "But you have turned it into a robbers' den."

The scrambling men and beasts were mixed up together as they tried to get away. The pilgrims were pleased at the misfortunes of the money-changers and some began to cheer. Nathan wanted to shout, too, because he saw that Jesus was cleansing the Temple of its enemies just as Judas Maccabeus had purified it so many years ago. Only, Nathan realized, this time it was his own people who were the enemies of the Temple.

The priests of the Temple who had seen and heard what had happened were not pleased like the pilgrims. They were very angry. Nathan could see some of them shaking their heads and talking loudly. Then they went hurrying off and Nathan wondered if they had gone to report to the High Priest. Anna put her hand to her breast. "Ah," she whispered, "they will not forgive that."

Jesus and his group were now moving away, and suddenly Nathan wanted to leave the Temple. He wanted to go home to Capernaum, home to the Sea of Galilee. He wanted Jesus to come back there where people were more gentle and kind. Nathan looked at the faces of the people who rushed by and those who were left. These people did not look like God's children. They were not the gentle, the pure in heart, or the makers of peace. They did not want goodness more than anything else. They were hungry for riches. They would never have that happiness which Jesus gave, which made people new. Jerusalem, a city of peace, thought Nathan, remembering how joyfully they had sung about it only the day before. There was no peace here! And there was no place for the Prince of Peace. There was more hate than love. How could God be worshiped where there was so much hate? The Kingdom of Heaven would not be found in this place.

Nathan caught his father's arm. "Can't we go, Father?" he begged. And seeing the terror in his face, Simeon led Nathan and Anna along the lofty aisles of the Court and through the crowd, which was now thinning out, until they came to a quiet spot on one of the other sides of the Temple. Nathan could look up and see the Roman soldiers keeping guard in a tower of the Roman fortress which overlooked the Temple courts. Their helmets glistened in the sunlight. They would use their swords if necessary to keep order during the Jewish feasts. They might be cruel to Jesus, Nathan thought. Jesus would not be afraid, he was sure of that now, but he felt he could not bear it if his dear friend were to fall into their hands.

Simeon was saying to Anna, "I think you were right about not coming this year. It would have been better to wait."

"But should we not stand together with him if he is in danger?" asked Anna.

Simeon shook his head. "He has made up his mind — there is nothing we can do, I am afraid."

"Made up his mind, Father?" asked Nathan, knowing they were speaking of Jesus and remembering the look he had seen on Jesus's face the day before.

"Yes," said Simeon proudly, looking across to the Mount of Olives, "he believes the Kingdom will not come until he has paid the price. And he means to do it."

"The price, Father?" Nathan pressed him. But Anna drew her scarf across her face and turned toward the gate.

"We shall see, my son," said Simeon.

That night it was decided that Anna and Nathan should not stay in Jerusalem for the feast. A Greek friend of Simeon's, who was traveling north through Capernaum, would see that they reached home safely and in time to eat their Passover supper with Enoch and Renah. It had been a hard decision for Simeon to make, and he had talked a long time with Anna and their relatives about it. Nathan had not heard what they were saying for Anna had given him a message to take to one of her friends in a near-by street. But, when he returned, he knew by their grave faces that there were reasons why this Passover season would be different from the usual celebration.

His heart was heavy when Simeon told him of the change in their plans. It meant the breakdown of all his hopes, but Jerusalem had become for him a hard and cruel city, and his father had said he could do nothing there for Jesus. Nathan did not say much as he and Anna prepared to turn their faces toward the north once more. Jesus, Nathan told himself, would come back to Galilee, to the people who were simple and loving. There he would be again the friend they had known and loved instead of that stern figure in the Temple. He would triumph over his enemies in Jerusalem.

It was a very different journey going home from the one Nathan had taken to Jerusalem. As they climbed to the top of the Mount of Olives, he looked back only once at the Holy City. There seemed now to be a hard glitter about the sunlight on its marble towers and palaces. Nathan knew the change was in his own feelings about it, for it was still a wonder city.

Nathan would live to see that city in the hands of its enemies and the Temple burned to the ground forty years later, but he never again felt about it as he had on the day he had first approached it crying "Hosanna!" with the multitude which proclaimed Jesus, Messiah. With his face finally turned toward his own city in Galilee, Nathan paused for a moment to cuddle the nose of his mother's donkey against his neck before leading him forward. Anna leaned down and put her hand lightly on his shoulder for an instant. Nathan knew she understood.

The Feast of Passover had been celebrated, and four more days had gone by when Simeon came one night into the courtyard of their home. He was back sooner than they had expected and Enoch and Nathan ran to meet him. Then they stopped short in surprise, for Simeon's shoulders were bent and he looked old and tired. Anna and Renah came to the door when they heard his step, and Anna went quickly to his side. "Come, sit down," she cried, taking Simeon's arm, "you are very tired."

Simeon let her lead him into the house and the children followed. Nathan knew, before his father spoke, what he would say. Something had happened to Jesus — something terrible!

"He died," said Simeon slowly, "on a cross."

"A cross!" Anna beat her hands together softly and wept. Nathan ran from the house and no one tried to stop him.

Almost blindly he took the path across the fields which he had taken that afternoon two years before when he had been trying to find the Healer. When he was breathless from running, he dropped to the ground beneath a twisted fig tree. The shadows were not so dark here as they were in the town, but Nathan had no room in his mind for fear of the wild animals which sometimes came down from the hills at night to prey upon the flocks of sheep or goats. His world was in pieces and nothing else seemed to matter. A boy of twelve could not cry even before his own family. But here, with his face buried in his arms, the sobs which had almost stopped his breathing as he ran, could burst against the scent of the warm earth and the flowers which his body was crushing. Only the birds that flew from nests in alarm as he fell could see his grief.

Jesus was dead. Jerusalem, the city of David, and the rulers of the Temple which he had been taught to love, had put him to death. They did not want his kingdom, and the only way they knew of destroying it was to destroy the king. The King! Nathan remembered how happy he had been on that day going up to Jerusalem, with everyone singing and crying "Hosanna!" to Jesus as the One whom God had sent to save them. But the rulers of the Temple would not receive him. They had killed him — just as Herod had killed John the Baptizer, and in a way that was used as a punishment for criminals!

Nathan dug his fingers deep into the grass. This was something he could not believe — yet it must be true. Jesus had not been afraid, he thought proudly. He did not run away. He *could* have. What was that his father had said in the Temple court? "He has made up his mind." Yes, he had. Nathan had seen that in his face, only — he hadn't known what Jesus had made up his mind to do, or he would have stayed and fought for him until he died, too. Nathan's thoughts ran on and on, but his sobbing grew quieter. He lifted his head and saw that the stars were already thick in the darkening sky. Then he heard his father's voice calling his name, and saw his figure coming along the path. Nathan got up and ran to him.

"I thought I should find you here," said Simeon. He held out his hand as though Nathan were not twelve years old, and Nathan was not ashamed to put his own into it. So they walked back home together, and as they went they talked quietly of Jesus.

"I think it is like this, Nathan," said Simeon. "You know how my brother, Benjamin, and all good shepherds put the safety of their sheep before their own safety? Some of them have given their lives to protect and defend their flocks from an enemy or a wild beast."

"Yes," said Nathan, thinking of how Benjamin had gone searching for the little lost lamb. He thought, too, of the story about David's killing the lion and bear when they had threatened his sheep.

Simeon went on: "It was like that with Jesus. He is the Good Shepherd, and we, who belong to the Kingdom, are the sheep and lambs of his fold. He had hoped he could bring the people of Jerusalem and the rulers of the Temple into that fold — we had all hoped for it — but, when they refused to accept his Good News of the Kingdom and so could not be brought into his fold, the Good Shepherd had to die to save the flock which was already there. He laid down his life that the wolves of pride and greed and selfishness might not creep in through the door of the sheepfold and destroy them."

Nathan understood that. He had seen shepherds lie down across the entrance to their sheepfolds at night. A good shepherd *would* die for his sheep. "But who will take the place of the Shepherd now?" he asked.

"I think, my son," answered Simeon, "that Jesus would not leave us without a shepherd. I believe it was for that he kept his twelve friends so constantly with him. He wanted to teach them to be shepherds of many flocks, and all will belong to him who is our great Shepherd. Even though he has gone from us, Nathan, we shall find him every place where there is kindness and love."

Nathan pressed close against his father's shoulder, letting the words of comfort sink deep into his heart. Surely God, whom Jesus had named Father, would care for His dear

Son. His Kingdom would grow, and Jesus would still be King in their hearts.

The next day Simeon took Nathan to the farm with him. The barley was ripe and ready for harvesting. Asa let Nathan drive the oxen and threshing cart over the threshing floor. It kept him busy and his heart felt lighter. He thought of how planting and harvesting happened over and over again, and he remembered God's promise in one of the Sacred Scrolls:

> "While the earth remaineth, seed-time and harvest,
> and cold and heat, and summer and winter, and day
> and night shall not cease."

Nathan repeated this aloud, and Asa, who was walking beside the cart, looked up and nodded. "God planned it that way," he said. "It is the law of all life, whether it is working in the seed under the ground or in the growing things above the ground, or . . ." Asa put out his hand to guide the oxen, and then went on, "or in man, Nathan. Nothing is lost. Man goes on and on, too."

After a moment Nathan said: "Jesus would go on and on, Asa, no matter what they did to him, wouldn't he?"

"Jesus most of all," said Asa, "for he is life itself, Nathan."

Toward evening Joseph came back to the farm. He threw himself down on husks of the barley which had been brushed into a pile after the good heads of the grain had been winnowed. Pilgrims were coming back from Jerusalem now, and Joseph said he had been with a caravan which had just reached Capernaum. Simeon, Asa, and Nathan were

183

resting after their day's work. Nathan was anxious to know. if Juda and Eber had been with them.

"I didn't see them," said Joseph. Then he turned to Simeon. "Peter and John have been telling a strange story about Jesus of Nazareth. They say the place where he was laid for burial was empty on the first day of the week. No one had been there during the Sabbath, but early on the first day of the week Mary of Magdala and Mary, the mother of James, went to the tomb and came running back with this story. Peter and John went themselves and say they found it true. I think they must all be out of their minds, but the stories are going around that Jesus is alive and has been seen by others." Joseph sat up suddenly. "What if it were true!" he said. And Nathan, whose heart had seemed to stop beating for a moment, saw in Joseph's face a new light of longing and love.

Simeon and Asa were asking Joseph questions, but he did not know any more than he had already told them. Nobody dared to say much on account of Herod and the rulers of the Temple. They did not want to get into trouble. The disciples themselves were keeping quiet. They were still in Jerusalem.

Then one day Peter's house was open again, and Nathan felt the same thrill and warmth in his heart when he saw it that he had known ever since Jesus had first stopped there. Nathan was on an errand for his mother, but he could not pass the house without pausing to see if Juda were around. He heard the voices of Sara and her mother, busy about their tasks, but Juda was not there. Nathan met him down on the shore. He was fishing with a net in the shallow water, but he came running when Nathan called.

They did not speak of Jerusalem. It was still too strange and terrible an experience for either of them to know what to say, and Nathan had a feeling that Jerusalem didn't matter much any more. There was a glad new hope in his heart that had taken the place of sadness and terror. Nathan saw the wonder of it in Juda's eyes, too, as they splashed about in the shallows. Nathan said he was helping on his father's farm. Perhaps Juda would like to help if his mother could spare him.

"That would be fun," said Juda, "unless my father should want my help with the fishing. He is coming home to Capernaum, Nathan. All will be going back to their homes now." Juda drew closer to Nathan and gripped his arm until it hurt. "Nathan," he said, "Jesus is alive!"

"Yes — I know!" answered Nathan. They stared at each other for a moment, then Nathan turned in a tumult of joy and raced up the shore with Juda after him. Their shouts made many an old fisherman, busy mending his nets, smile and long for his own boyhood days.

Peter came home not many days later. Nathan's father went often to his house, and James and John came over from Bethsaida. Matthew, and others of the Twelve also came and went. Sometimes there were groups meeting at Nathan's house, and he would sit in a quiet corner where he could hear them as they talked about the Kingdom. It seemed as though all had the feeling of being ready — like a caravan waiting only for the leader to give the word to start. Or —

and Nathan liked this thought — like watchmen on the
mountains waiting for a signal. He remembered his father
telling him that in olden times they had lighted beacon fires
on the hills to show the time of the Passover moon. The
lovely singing words of the prophet Isaiah came into his
mind.

> "How beautiful upon the mountains are the feet
> of him that bringeth good tidings; that publisheth peace;
> . . . .
>
> that saith unto Zion, Thy God reigneth.
> Thy watchmen shall lift up the voice."

Were they the watchmen, waiting for the Prince of Peace
to announce his Kingdom and give them the signal? It would
not be the signal to start toward Jerusalem, Nathan was
thinking. It would mean turning their faces toward another
city. He was remembering that look he had seen on Jesus's
face as he had looked across to Jerusalem from the Mount
of Olives. Nathan had thought it was as though he were
seeing a *far* city. Perhaps — it was the Holy City of the
Kingdom of God that Jesus had been seeing. That was it —
the *New* Jerusalem — a city where God would reign.

One morning Nathan wakened very early. It was still
dark, but he thought he could see, when he raised his head,
an air of expectancy on the hills across the lake — as though
they were getting ready to welcome the sun. He was no
longer sleepy and his feet itched for the cool water which
would be making little frothy patterns on the shore. With-

out disturbing anyone, he stole down the steps to the courtyard and slipped through the quiet streets to the lake.

He could see the dark shadows of boats at anchor or
drawn up to the quays. Nathan waded a few inches into
the water and loved the feeling of tiny waves lapping against
his ankles. He looked for Peter's boat, but it was not in its
familiar place. Nathan thought he must be mistaken because
Peter had not gone fishing since his return from Jerusalem.
He walked along the shore looking for the boat, but he
could not see it. Perhaps Peter had gone out the night before.

Nathan walked on, kicking up little showers of spray
around his legs. His eyes still searched the water. At last,
off a quiet cove, he saw a boat not far from the shore. There
were several men in the boat, and, although the dawn had
not yet come, Nathan could tell Peter because of his size.
Peter was pulling in his drag-net. It seemed to cost him no
effort, so Nathan knew there were few if any fish in it. The
surface of the lake was still, and the men in the boat with
Peter were not moving about. There was an appearance of
being discouraged, Nathan thought, as though they had
been fishing all night and had caught nothing.

The flare of a small fire farther down the beach caught
Nathan's eyes. He wondered if one of the fishermen had
come ashore to cook breakfast for the others. Perhaps it
was Juda. Nathan started to run closer, then he stopped.
No — that was a man, he decided. A moment later he heard
the man calling to the fishermen. Nathan thought he must
be telling them to try the net on the other side of the boat,
for they all seemed to take a hand in changing the clumsy

net to the far side. One or two acted as though it were not much use. Then, suddenly, they were all grasping and tugging at the net, their backs bent with the weight of it. All at once Peter left them and sprang into the water, splashing toward the shore like a great fish himself. Nathan was too surprised for a few minutes to do or think of anything except what was happening to Peter and the others. Then his heart began to thump. He saw Peter reach the beach and stand dripping before that other dim figure. Suddenly Nathan knew whose voice he had heard.

The other fishermen were coming ashore in a small boat, dragging their net after them in the water so it would not sink the boat. Nathan went back from the water and crept a little closer, keeping in the deeper shadow of the date palm trees. He knew, as he had known that day on the hills back of Capernaum, that this moment was for Jesus and his disciples alone. But his love held him hidden there, with no thought of anything more than to hear the beloved voice again.

A smell of fish cooking on the fire blew with the wood smoke into Nathan's nostrils. Jesus had been cooking breakfast for the fishermen! That was like him. The men sat down and ate, with only the light of the fire on their faces. Once when the fire flared up and the light fell with special brightness upon Jesus, Nathan saw with joy that his face had again the familiar calm and tender lines that had made it dear to so many people. All the strange, stern look of those sad days in Jerusalem was gone. Nathan thought Jesus was probably enjoying the surprise he had given Peter, James,

Nathan, Boy of Capernaum

John and the rest. They were speaking in low tones, but suddenly Jesus asked a question which Nathan heard quite well. It rang out in the still morning air like a bell. Jesus had asked Peter if he loved him! Peter's voice showed his astonishment as he answered: "You know I love you!" There was a pause, then Nathan heard Jesus say: "Feed my lambs."

Twice again Jesus asked Peter the same question, and Nathan thought the last time, as Peter answered "You know all things, Master, you know I love you!" that in Peter's voice was so much longing to make Jesus understand how great his love was, that it was like a cry. For the second time Jesus told Peter to feed his sheep. Nathan remembered what his father had said about Jesus being the great Shepherd and having other shepherds to care for his flocks. Perhaps that was why Jesus told Peter so many times to feed his lambs and sheep. He wanted to be sure that Peter was ready to do his work. Nathan put his head down and buried his face in his arms. He could not hear words now, but the sound of Jesus's voice still reached him. He felt the same joy in just listening to that voice as he had the first time he had heard it.

A ray of sunlight flashed across the hills and found its way under Nathan's eyelids. He realized the dawn had come. He wanted, so much, to creep up and join that group around the fire. Only to say his name or get one smile from Jesus. Only to sit there quietly without once opening his lips. But Nathan knew he could not do it. This, perhaps, was the signal to the "watchmen." Could it be his signal, too? Nathan wondered as he got up and ran along the shore toward home.

The King of Love

Jesus would never be far away, he would always be coming back as he had said. And it didn't so much matter about seeing him as long as you were doing his work and would not be ashamed if he did come.

As he reached the place where he must turn into the city, Nathan stopped and looked across the lake which the sun had now transformed into a mirror for the sky. He would always, thought Nathan, see Jesus in the fishing boats and among fishermen. He remembered how Jesus had said to Peter long ago that he would make him a "fisher of men." Now Jesus had made Peter a shepherd, who should feed his sheep. Nathan laughed. It was that way with Jesus. He loved fishermen and shepherds and he knew how to make them understand by speaking of the things they were used to in their daily tasks. Jesus loved farmers, too, farmers like Simeon and Asa. Nathan knew he would see Jesus on the farm and in the hills. Yes, and in the market place or the synagogue. Why, there wasn't a spot that wouldn't speak to him of Jesus.

Then Nathan's thoughts flew to the far places which lay beyond the circle of hills that girdled his own home, and it came to him that the Good News of the Kingdom was not for his land alone, nor even for his own people. They couldn't keep it just for themselves. It must go to the ends of the earth. Maybe Jesus wanted Peter to understand that, too, when he said three times to feed his lambs and sheep. There were so many directions in which to look for lost sheep and bring them into the fold.

Nathan turned slowly to the north, then around to the

west, then south, and again to the east where the colors on the hills and valleys of this ever lovely land of Galilee were flaming forth in patches of red and gold. He was lost for a moment in the wonder of the world around him. Would Peter and the other friends of Jesus some day climb these hills and journey to far countries to carry the message of Jesus to people of different colors and races? Would there be other "watchmen" waiting for them to come so they, too, could carry it even farther?

Would there be beacon fires set on thousands of hills to give the signal for the coming of the King? The signal, thought Nathan, would be for women and children as well as for men. Women, like his mother, who were loving and wise; and children, like Juda, Eber, and himself — or Enoch — who, Jesus had said, were important to his Kingdom. Everyone who loved Jesus would have a part. Jesus had asked Peter if he loved him before he told him what to do.

Love, then, was the signal. Nathan felt happiness, like a bright flame, quicken within him, and he knew that the signal fire was burning in his own heart. He stretched out his arms and lifted himself on his toes, breathing in all the sun-drenched air his lungs could hold. It was, thought Nathan, almost as though he could see the far places of the earth and hear the sound of the feet of those who would carry the Good News of the Kingdom across the world.

"Master," he whispered, "I, too, will be your messenger."